Bridget Wilder
Spy-in-
Training

Bridget Wilder
Spy-in-Training

Jonathan Bernstein

KATHERINE TEGEN BOOKS
An Imprint of HarperCollins Publishers

Katherine Tegen Books is an imprint of HarperCollins Publishers.

Bridget Wilder: Spy-in-Training
Library of Congress Cataloging-in-Publication Data
Bernstein, Jonathan.
    Bridget Wilder, spy-in-training / Jonathan Bernstein. — First edition.
        pages   cm
    Summary: "An adopted middle child receives an unexpected package on an
otherwise unremarkable birthday inviting her to join a super-secret division of
the CIA"— Provided by publisher.
    ISBN 978-0-06-238266-5 (hardback)
    [1. Spies—Fiction.   2. Family life—Fiction.   3. Middle-born children—
Fiction.   4. Adoption—Fiction.]   I. Title.
PZ7.B4566Br 2015   2014047819
[Fic]—dc23   CIP
                                                                 AC

        15 16 17 18 19   CG/RRDH   10 9 8 7 6 5 4 3 2 1
                                    ❖
                            First Edition

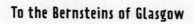
To the Bernsteins of Glasgow

CHAPTER ONE

Invisible

When I fell asleep last night I was still twelve. A child. A barely formed person. A blank slate. Now I'm awake and I'm thirteen. I've changed. I can't put my finger on exactly how. I just know I feel different.

"Bridge."

Maybe it's the confidence that comes with age. Maybe there's something special about me that's always been there but is only now ready to emerge like a butterfly crawling out of its cocoon.

"Bridget!"

I wonder if my family will notice. I wonder if they're

as excited about this big birthday as I am.

"BRIDGET!"

Wait, that's my brother's voice! My older-in-years-but-not-maturity brother, Ryan. Is he outside the house and waking me up to sing "Happy Birthday" to me?

I grope for my glasses, roll out of bed, and yank open the curtains to see my brother, my unshaven, disheveled brother, perched on the top rung of our rarely used ladder. He's grinning at me like waking up to find him inches from my window ledge is an everyday occurrence. He gestures to me to open the window. I peer at the clock. Six fifty-five a.m. I ought to jump back into bed, pull the covers and possibly a pillow over my head, turn on the radio, and leave him out there. But it's six fifty-five a.m. and he's standing on a ladder outside my bedroom window. I must know why!

I open the window and the gangly idiot crawls in. He goes to pat my head and I recoil in horror. He smells like old wood, rust, and paint. It's the smell of our dank little garden shed, where we keep the ladder. I want to be cool here. I fold my arms, shake my head slightly, and let the hint of a smile play across my lips. I want him to understand he's the screw-up and I'm the awesome sibling. The one who's wise beyond her years.

"What are you doing? You're grounded," I squeak,

sounding every bit the freaked-out little sister. He just gives me his signature stupid grin and a half-asleep look. "You can't cage the kid," he yawns, dragging a hand through his unruly black hair. "Try to cage the kid, the kid'll break out of the cage." Then he tracks dirt across my nice clean room and tumbles onto my bed!

"Ryan, get up!" But he doesn't get up. He rolls into a ball with his dirty sneakers on my actual comforter.

"The kid needs his sleep," he mutters.

"Of course the kid . . . of course *you're* sleepy," I reply, trying to keep my voice low and unsqueaky. "You were out all night. What did you do? Where did you go? Who were you with?"

"I'll tell you when you're older."

"I *am* older." I wait for this to sink in. I wait for the look of realization. I wait for Ryan to be the first to congratulate me on my special day.

"I *am* older," I repeat.

Nothing. He just lies there infesting my bedsheets with fungus and mold.

"Like how you used to be fifteen and then you turned sixteen?"

More nothing. Just the sound of his congested breathing. Is he messing with me?

"Are those Christmas lights?" he suddenly says.

I follow his baffled gaze to the strings of colorful bulbs framing my door and windows.

"What's up with that? Christmas is seven months away."

Now it's my turn to look baffled. "Have we been formally introduced? You know I like them on all year round. It's my thing. One of my things."

But even as I'm saying this, I'm thinking, *Ryan never comes in here. He doesn't know what my things are. He barely knows me.* Which is why he chose my room to sneak back into the house. Anywhere else he'd leave a dirty trail. His own bedroom window has long been superglued shut in a futile effort to keep him from doing whatever it is he keeps doing. But no one would ever think of looking for him in here. Ryan shakes his head and favors me with a condescending smirk. "That's a little bit disturbed."

"You stole a car. You've got the disturbed category all sewn up."

"I was *in* a car that was stolen by someone else," he says, all innocent. "I was a victim."

"You drove to Vegas."

"I was a victim in Vegas."

"Mom and Dad have talked about sending you to military school. Dad bookmarked the home page."

"Awesome. Teach the kid hand-to-hand combat. Give him access to loaded weapons. Dream come true."

Then we both hear it. Loud. Harsh. Painful and sustained. Dad's first nose blow of the morning, echoing around the house from three rooms away. We lock eyes. This could go several ways. The nose blow could lead to a bout of hacking coughs, which could lead to a visit to the bathroom. A visit to the bathroom inevitably leads to a shout of, "If I'm up, everybody's up!" Which means a thump, or group of thumps, on the door.

Ryan puts a finger to his lips. He slides off the comforter and attempts to squeeze under the bed.

We wait in silence, anticipating the follow-up cough. An eternity passes. But there is no further phlegm to be expelled.

"Ryan," I whisper. "The mole is back in his hole. Repeat, the mole is back in his hole."

In reply, three sharp high musical notes sound from under my bed.

For a second I think, *He's playing along. He's whistling like it's our secret code.* Then there's a bunch of tuneless peeping and I realize the worst thing that could possibly happen has happened. *Ryan has found my flute.*

Sure enough, Ryan rolls out from under the bed with a delighted look on his face and my silver-plated closed-hole C flute in his hands.

"Put that back," I demand.

"What's this?" He laughs.

I could remind him. I could say, "Remember I was in the school band last year? Remember I played at the Christmas concert?" I could go on, "Oh no, you don't remember. 'Cause you weren't there. That was the night you got caught trying to abduct a red fox from the zoo. Which meant that Mom and Dad weren't there, either." Instead I say, "It's not yours. Put it away." I can feel my face reddening. He does not do as I ask. Instead he wheezes into the flute some more. I make a grab for it. He holds it up over my head. "You want it back? Here it is," he says. I'm not going to jump up like a dog trying to grab a Frisbee. I'm not going to do it.

"I thought you wanted it back. Look, here it is," he says. He lowers the flute. I try to take it. Once again, he holds it out of my reach. I jump.

"I hate you so much," I seethe.

My scarlet face and furious words only seem to make him happier. And then we hear music. Not terrible flute music. Actual real melodic music. It's coming from a few rooms away. It's that Katy Perry song where she asks if you ever feel like a plastic bag.

Ryan tosses the flute onto my bed. "The little sister

machine is up," he says. "Which gives the kid thirty seconds to beat her to the bathroom. Thus creating the impression he's in a hurry to get to school. 'Cause the kid's a reformed character."

Ryan holds out a hand to be high-fived. When he sees I have no intention of congratulating him for his web of lies and deceit, he *high-fives himself*! And with that, he's out the door and gone.

A matter of seconds later, I hear his feet pounding on the carpet. I hear a high-pitched voice wail, *"Ryan!"* I hear Ryan's voice shout, "Kid's gotta jam." And I hear the bathroom door slam shut.

"He's *so* annoying," sighs my younger sister, Natalie, as she walks into my room. Her eyebrows shoot up when she sees the flute lying on top of my bed. "You've got a flute," she says, gazing at me with big blue eyes. "Why didn't you tell me? We can play duets. Woodwind sounds beautiful with acoustic guitar." I say nothing. I don't have to. Natalie picks up on my reluctance (although she doesn't pick up on my fear of being upstaged). "I understand," she says, nodding. "Music's so personal. But I can't wait to hear you play. I just know it'll be beautiful."

You know when you see a parent who's totally lost control of a kid? Like in the street or in a supermarket and the kid's all red-faced and screaming and the parent's shushing the kid and apologizing to everyone who passes and the kid's only getting louder and more obnoxious? You know how there's always *another* kid, across the road or in the next aisle, who's perfect? Quiet and calm and well behaved. An absolute angel. And the flustered parent sees the perfect kid and then looks back at their own howling monster and thinks, *I want that one. I want to change my bad kid for that good one.* Natalie's the good one. Look at her now, heading toward me with a smile on her cute little face, holding a pink envelope in her outstretched hand.

"I was going to slide this under your door," she says. "But that didn't feel right."

This is how my special day was supposed to start. I thank my lovely little sister, open the envelope, remove and unfold the contents, and read about the dance charity marathon taking place in two weeks. I guess I was dwelling on the lack of birthday card or gift and missed the part where she stopped talking because Natalie's staring at me with a quizzical look on her face. "So, what do you want to do?" she says. "How do you want to help?" Without waiting for my response, she carries on. "You could sell T-shirts or man the refreshments table. But it'll be fun. And I bet you'll make some friends." I don't even flinch as the dagger of sympathy slips between my shoulder blades. "Thanks," says Natalie. "You're the best." And with that, the sweetest, most caring and compassionate eleven-year-old girl in the entire state of California leaves me alone.

Okay. So, no birthday acknowledgment from older brother or younger sister. Two more family members to go.

"The locking tab" are the first words I hear my mother speak as I make my appearance in the kitchen. She rolls her eyes at me and gestures disgustedly at the phone. "I'm talking to someone in Bangalore," she groans. I linger by her side for a moment in the hope my presence will motivate her to hang up and devote all her attention to me and my once-a-year celebration. Speaking slowly and patiently, my mother tells the customer service representative on the other end of the phone, "The locking tab didn't lock. Which meant the processor didn't work. I sent you back the locking tab. You sent me the replacement. But it didn't come with the feed tube. Without the feed tube, the new locking tab is as useless as the old locking tab." She makes a claw of her hand and mimes a throttling gesture.

I give up lingering and pour myself a bowl of Frosted Flakes. And because I'm a year older, because my tastes are changing and maturing, I decide to slice up some strawberries and add them to my cereal. "One, two, three, four," I say as I cut up the first strawberry. "Five, six, seven, eight." I drop the next bunch of sliced-up fruit into the bowl. "Nan, check this out," yells my dad from the living room. "Nine, ten, eleven," I continue, raising my voice as I slice and plop.

"Come and look at this thing," Dad says, entering the kitchen.

Mom waves him off. "I've already given you the serial number," she says into the phone.

"Twelve, thirteen," I say, as loud as I can without actually breaking into a shout. "*Thirteen* slices." Mom makes a shushing gesture. "Is thirteen enough?" I ask. "Is that a good number for me?" Dad reaches into my bowl and grabs a handful of sliced-up strawberries. I stare at him in horror.

"Gross and rude!"

"I know," nods Dad as he crunches dry cereal and swallows my carefully calculated strawberry slices. "Learn by example. Never behave like that. It's unacceptable." He gives me a big stupid grin that is *exactly* like the big stupid grin Ryan uses to get away with everything.

"So," I say, putting my hands on my hips. "Do you have anything else you want to say to me? Anything that might make today even more special than it already is?"

He thinks about it for a second. *You actually have to think about it? You're either an award-winning actor or an unfit father!*

Mom drops her phone on the kitchen island and exhales in frustration.

Dad stops thinking about my very important question and grabs her hand.

"Come and see this," he says. "It's an infomercial for that thing Harmon in Accounts was talking about. The thing for his back. The inversion table."

"Did you just hear me on the phone? That's going to be you. Don't order anything with parts."

"Harmon said it saved his back. You know the state my back's in. It needs to be saved."

Mom allows herself to be dragged from the kitchen. I am once again alone. Well, not totally alone. The kitchen cabinet door nearest to me swings open. "Kitchen ghost," I mutter to myself. That's what we call the errant door that randomly flies open of its own accord. There's no name for the burned-out light inside the fridge that's never been fixed. Or the faucet that keeps dripping no matter how tight it's squeezed. Or the rattling sound from the stove. They're just facts of life. I think I might miss them if Mom or Dad ever got around to fixing them. I almost feel like they're part of the family.

I look around the kitchen. Pictures of the Wilder clan from Reindeer Crescent, Sacramento, are taped to the fridge door and nailed to the walls. The parents seem like a fun, pleasant-looking couple. The older brother is making the pretty younger sister laugh in almost all the pictures. And then there's the girl in the middle. The one they adopted when they found out the mom wasn't going to be able to have any more kids. They obviously liked her. They wouldn't have put themselves through the whole adoption process otherwise. Or maybe they just didn't want to be stuck alone with Ryan. But then, much to the astonishment of modern medicine, Natalie, the completely unexpected miracle baby, fell out of the sky and into their lives. Which doesn't mean they cared any less for the girl they'd adopted. It just means there was more of a demand for their attention.

I've seen these fridge door pictures a thousand times but today might be the first time I've ever *really* looked at them. I seem like some passerby who blundered in front of the camera. I don't belong at all. Ryan's a devil. Natalie's an angel. And me, I'm just staring off to the side. All of a sudden, I find myself thinking about my birth parents. I was ten when Mom and Dad told me I was adopted. They asked me if I wanted them to try and find my real parents. The usual daydreams about being the heir to the throne of Luxembourg or the secret love child of Stephen Colbert whirled around my head. But I declined. My biologicals chose not to participate in the wonder of me. I don't entertain fantasies about them realizing the error of their ways and begging me to let them back into my life. But I'm wondering if they're thinking about me today.

Okay, ease up on the self-pity, I tell myself. *Have the Wilders ever missed a birthday before? No. They're planning something special. And this? This is fun. This is them working hard to make you think they've forgotten. So play along and act surprised when they break into "Happy Birthday."*

I hear a peal of delighted girlie laughter from the living room. Ha! Lovely little Natalie couldn't keep up the facade. She's been aching to hug me and tell me I'm the best sister anyone's ever had. I decide to let her off the hook.

I hurry into the living room. Lovely little Natalie is shaking with delighted laughter as she shows Ryan her hip-hop moves and he tries clumsily to copy them. Mom and Dad are gazing rapt at the TV as the guy onscreen hangs upside down chained to a table. Mom turns to Dad and shakes her head. "It's a miracle," he protests. "It's a deathtrap," she replies. Dad argues back. Ryan grabs Natalie and throws her over his shoulder. She shrieks in giggling horror as he dances her around the room.

No one notices me. I stand and watch my mom, my dad, my brother and sister arguing and shrieking and giggling and dancing for a moment. I suddenly feel like the kitchen ghost, the dead fridge light, the dripping faucet, and the rattling stove might be more a part of the family than I am.

Okay, stop easing up on the self-pity, I tell myself. *They've forgotten your birthday.*

CHAPTER TWO

Where Nobody Knows Your Name

Despite Natalie's implication, I do, in fact, have a friend. Her name is Joanna Conquest. She lives two blocks from me. Her block differs from mine in the number of xeroxed missing-dog posters stapled to trees and telephone poles. My block has fewer lost pets but more sidewalk space devoted to abandoned cardboard boxes filled with unsellable trinkets left over from weekly yard sales. Other than that, they're identical. Houses that could do with a fresh coat of paint. Lawns that could use more frequent trims. Family cars that could use a wash.

I meet Joanna on this warm spring day, like I do

every weekday morning, as she walks down her driveway. She wears a shapeless blue smock. I complement her in a shapeless blue tracksuit. She greets me, like she does every weekday morning, by starting a monologue that requires no response or participation from me.

"Earthquake alert," she bellows, as she falls into step with me and we begin the trudge to school. "People are trembling. They're shivering in fear. And why? Because I've revised and updated the Conquest Report."

The Conquest Report is Joanna's Tumblr. It has one follower. Guess who?

"Big changes. If you were happy you didn't make the cut last time, sorry to burst your bubble. If I didn't mention you by name, it probably only means I didn't notice you. But I've got big eyes . . ."

This is actually untrue. Joanna has tiny little eyes, like Raisinets. And chubby scarlet cheeks. Which might lead you to the initial impression that she's fun. Fun and jolly and generous and bighearted. But your initial impression would be incorrect.

". . . and whatever you hid from me before, your loud screechy voice, your nervous laugh, your toxic breath, I've noticed it. I've noticed it and it irritates me. It irritates me enough to add you to my ever-expanding list of people I hate. Kelly Beach. Keep bragging about your stepdaddy's software empire, Kel. *Don't* stop just because he's seconds away from bankruptcy . . ."

Joanna continues to rant in this fashion. I continue to stay silent. Our friendship remains now as it was seven years ago when my mother and her grandmother saw us sitting sullen and alone at a neighborhood Christmas party.

"Bridget," smiled my mother. "Why don't you and Joanna play together?"

"Joanna," said her grandmother. "Why don't you and that girl play together?"

After several moments of awkward, tiny-eyed, chubby-cheeked silence, Joanna started talking about the other kids at the party. The ones who annoyed her because they were too clingy. The ones who smelled weird. The ones who were covered in cat hair. But, as Joanna continued heaping ever-higher spoonfuls of disdain, I looked around the party and I couldn't really see anyone who fit her description. All the kids she labeled losers seemed like they were having fun. I found myself wishing I was hanging out with those other kids, even if they had speech defects or couldn't control their bladders. At one point, I remember catching my mother's eye. She gave me a little wink, which, due to our intuitive mother-daughter bond, I knew meant she was glad I'd made the effort and any minute now we were going to make an exit from the party and head home. And a half hour later, we did. Which was when Mom said, "Looks like you made yourself a BFF." For a second, I had no clue what she was talking about. Then I did. I don't know what was more shattering: discovering there was no such thing as our intuitive mother-daughter bond, or realizing I was about to get stuck with a whole lot of Joanna. Our relationship, such as it is, may be one bad playdate that never ended. But on days like today when I feel horribly let down, when I feel like no one in the world gets me, I'm glad I know her.

"So," I say as she takes a breath between listing all the new targets of her scorn. "They forgot my birthday."

Joanna squints her tiny eyes at me. Her lips part. And then any further expression of surprise vanishes from her face. She shrugs the backpack straps off her shoulder and reaches inside her red L.L. Bean bag. A moment later, she thrusts a book at me.

"Happy birthday," she says.

I'm touched. I'm taken aback. I'm surprised. I look at the book. *The Diary of a Young Girl* by Anne Frank. A dog-eared, second—maybe-even-third—hand copy. The name *Sarah B* is scrawled on the top left-hand corner. I'm disappointed. But not *hideously*. I've got a good idea of the sort of stuff Joanna keeps in that bag. I could have been stuck with the black banana or her half-empty, crusted-over bottle of hair dye.

"Thanks, Joanna," I say. "I always wanted to read Anne Frank's diary." I mean it, too. I would have liked a new copy, one that didn't have all its page corners folded by Sarah B and wasn't defaced with scrawls of *I am bored x 1000*. "She was so brave."

Joanna clicks her tongue. "She was annoying. And you know who else is annoying . . . ?" My birthday celebration is apparently over.

When I reach Reindeer Crescent Middle School, jewel in the crown of Southern California's education system, I'm greeted by the marching band who break into a stirring rendition of "Happy Birthday to You." And what's this? The whole school is joining in. The Cheerminators are flipping and bouncing in my honor. The lunch ladies wheel my cake toward me. It takes four of them to move it. That's a big cake.

JK! J totally K. I can K because, in this instance, I expect nothing. As far as Reindeer Crescent is concerned, I might as well be invisible. As far as Reindeer Crescent is concerned, Joanna might as well be invisible, too. But she deals with that reality in a different way.

"Look at Casey Breakbush—look at the way she's

cowering away from me. I see you, girl, I see you wondering whether I showed mercy and left you off the Conquest Report. But guess what, Casey? Today, just like the day you decided all your problems would be over after your parents splashed out on ankle-fat reduction surgery, is not your lucky day." Slim, pretty, Casey Breakbush is neither cowering nor showing any indication she is aware of Joanna's existence. But the second I walk into Room A117 for my first class, someone is aware of mine.

"Making her way into the arena, give it up for Midget Wilder!"

Don't go red, I tell myself. I fail to follow my own orders and feel the tingle spread across my face and neck.

"Watch out! Don't accidentally step on the midget!"

I do what I always do when Brendan Chew launches into his stand-up routine. I shake my head in disgust, roll my eyes, and invite the rest of the class to share my contempt. I don't actually say the words but I think my expression makes my feelings plain: *You're going to sit there and endure this dork, this skinny, buck-toothed, acne-spattered clown, as he makes the same pathetic, unimaginative, embarrassing joke day after day? The same joke that isn't even factually accurate. I'm far from a midget. Dwarfism is defined as an adult height of four foot ten inches. I'm considerably taller than that. So basically Chew was able to find a word that rhymes with my name. And you're going to vali-date his tragic existence by laughing?*

They are. They do. They all laugh. Apparently call-ing me Midget Wilder is one of those jokes that *just keeps getting funnier.* I shoot a *Help me!* look at Joanna. She's laughing! That tiny-eyed traitor is chuckling to herself. Her extra chin is wobbling with the hilarity of it all.

"He's in the report, right?" I hiss at her.

She shrugs. "He's funny."

It's lunchtime. I'm eating a white peach frozen yogurt and flipping through my defaced birthday book in the fro-yo store around the corner from the school. Yes, that is cor-rect. I'm sitting in a booth by myself eating yogurt and reading Anne Frank's diary. *On my birthday.* Stood up by my one friend. (She texted me she was meeting an anonymous tipster who had some molten-hot scoop for the Report. Which I took to mean she feared she would be expected to buy me lunch.) Nothing remotely pathetic about that.

I was going to purchase a protein bar from the Big Green Machine, the new and widely despised healthy-food vending machine recently installed outside the gym by Vice Principal Scattering, who loves it like a new-born child. But, just like every day, I decided against it—although I did not decide to kick the machine as I passed it, which is how the majority of my fellow students express their feelings toward our Big Green friend—and chose to take my birthday lunch outside school property. Actually, white peach is my favorite flavor and the parts of the book Sarah B has left unfolded and un-scribbled-over are drawing me in.

I look up from the book and glance out the window. Dale Tookey approaches. That's "uncoordinated, asthmatic, untrustworthy Dale Tookey," according to the Conquest Report. I do not agree with Joanna's assessment. He seems all right to me. Maybe more than all right. He has a nice smile. I know because he smiled at me once. It might not have been *at* me. But I saw it so I choose to believe it was intended for me. Anyway, that doesn't matter. What matters is, I don't particularly want someone, even someone with a nice smile, to catch me alone with my yogurt and my defaced classic. What if he tried to talk to me? Unlikely, I admit. But I feel myself getting flustered again just thinking about it. What if he totally ignored me? Then my fragile illusion that he'd smiled at me would crumble to dust. I don't make things easy for myself, do I? As I see it, my only option is to flee to the restroom and hide out until he purchases his fro-yo and departs.

Excellent plan, Bridget. Nothing remotely pathetic about that.

I start to slide out of the booth. That's when I hear the raised voices and the metal clanking on the sidewalk. I peer out the window. Four guys. Big guys. Older. Fifteen, sixteen. Wearing basketball jerseys, baseball caps, and hoodies with the letters D and P graffitied on the sleeves. They're kicking cans in the street, shouting something in unison. I can't make it out at first. But as they keep up the chant, it starts to get clearer. It sounds like they're yelling *Doom Patrol* over and over. Their voices go up on the *Doom*; they come down on the *Patrol*. It's nice that they rehearse.

They come to a halt a few feet outside the entrance of the fro-yo store. I don't see what happens next. But I hear loud, harsh laughter. And I see Dale go staggering backward. I see him trying not to look scared. The four guys surround him. They're up in his face, crowding him, shoving him, yelling, "Doom Patrol!" His face is getting redder. He's trying to hold it together. To show them they're not getting to him. I feel sick just watching this. I can't imagine how Dale Tookey must feel. Finally, he thrusts a hand in his pocket and pulls out a crumpled wad of dollar bills. One of them snatches it from his hand. While he does this, another grabs Dale's backpack, opens it, and empties it in the street. Then they walk away, laughing loudly, shouting "Doom Patrol!" over and over.

I watch Dale as he squats down and tries to gather up all his stuff. I want to go and help. But even from this distance, I can see the look on his face. He's embarrassed and angry and close to tears. I slump back down in the booth. I feel awful for him and I feel stupid. I should have done something. I don't know what: yelled at them to leave him alone, taken pictures of them to send to the cops, thrown my yogurt at them? Would it have made any difference? Would the outcome have been any less humiliating for Dale? I doubt it. But I should have done *something*. Maybe I deserve to be alone on my birthday.

I wish I had an extracurricular activity or a group of friends to hang out with, or even a job. But I don't currently have any of these things. So I go home. Where no one will be there to greet me. Where FedEx will have delivered no packages with my name on them. Where no birthday cards will wait for me. Where no HAPPY BIRTHDAY, BRIDGET banners will stretch out to greet me. Mom and Dad are at work. Mom's in charge of a courier company, Wheel GetIt2u. (Think about it.) Dad manages the local Pottery Barn. (They were looking for someone who owned a messy house where nothing works.) Natalie's got soccer practice, then she's rehearsing for her role in the school musical she helped write, and after that she volunteers with Sacramento Animal Rescue. And Ryan? Who knows. Hostage situation. High-speed car chase. Aircraft hijack. But at least he's got a life. *What do I have?* I ask myself as I trudge up the driveway to the house. "Oh," I say out loud when I see the unexpected object with my name on it sitting on the doormat. "I've got a bag."

CHAPTER THREE

Goody Bag

It's a shopping bag. But it's not just *any* shopping bag. It's the sort of posh shopping bag you expect to see dangling from the arm of someone who spends their days and credit cards on Rodeo Drive. It's covered in brown and pink stripes. The handles are made from thickly braided black string. I cannot believe how excited I am. I can literally feel my heart beat as I get close to the bag. It actually takes an effort to restrain myself from jumping up and down and clapping my hands. *Which is totally what I want to do.*

I open the door, take the stairs at a gallop, charge into

my room, plop down on the bed, and peek into the bag.

Stuff!

There's *stuff* in the bag.

Presents. And an envelope.

Relief and guilt wash over me. Why would my family torment me like this? But why would I not trust them to come through for me? It's a complex issue, which . . . *Oh my God, they got me an iPhone!*

I yank the black rectangle from the bag. Who should I call first? Joanna? ("You know who's next to go in the Report? People who think their phones are awesome!") Perhaps not. Mom. I try to call Mom but there are no icons. No buttons to touch. Just a black screen. I look inside the bag for a charger. Nothing. I get it. I'm going to have to endure a lecture about how the phone is not free, how I can't call my friends in Zimbabwe, how I'll have to agree to use it responsibly before Mom and Dad will acti-vate it. So annoying. But still, I've got an awesome phone! And an envelope. I tear it open and find myself holding a card inviting me to a sale. A special invitation-only sale at a clothes store named Image Unlimited. Or, as it says on the card, IMAGE UNLTD. It promises me up to 50 percent off selected items. This must be Natalie's caring and compassionate way of calling me a slob who slobs around in slobby tracksuits.

What else is in my brown-and-pink treasure chest? Lip balm. A yellow tube of smoky pear–flavored lip balm. I try to pull the top off. It's stuck fast. Thanks, Ryan. Thanks for keeping the family tradition of worthless joke gifts alive. Funny it's the only tradition you remember to keep alive. But thanks, anyway. There's more. Tic Tacs. Green Tic Tacs. My unfavorite candy. Dad. This is where Ryan gets his incredible sense of humor. And just to prove that I can take a joke, my first call on my new phone *will* be to Zimbabwe. And it'll be an all-nighter. Ha!

Is there more? There's more. I pull out a glasses case, open it, and find a pair of glasses. Thick, severe, black-rimmed glasses. To make me look like even more of a dork and target for Brendan Chew's abuse? Or to create the illusion that I am a smart person capable of deep thoughts? I think Mom might be behind this present. I remove my oval wire frames and slip the new glasses on. Everything's a blur. These lenses aren't my prescription. Yeah, that mother-daughter bond was *totally* a figment of my imagination. What else? A USB thumb drive. Who cares? Finally, I reach inside the bag and fish out . . . keys. A set of keys. I jangle them from my fingertip. A car? My mind races. A secondhand car they're restoring in time for my sixteenth birthday? No way. But maybe.

I think back to Christmas three years ago, when Dad was all gloomy and he said times were hard, the economy was in trouble, and we'd have to make sacrifices. And then he woke us up on Christmas Eve and drove us to the airport, where we got on a flight to Hawaii. Fantastic! And a total surprise. He completely faked us out. So I'm thinking: Are the icky green Tic Tacs this year's hard times and tight belt? I think they are. At this moment, I could not love my devious dad more. And then I hear the low rumble of his voice from downstairs and I realize I'm wrong. I love him a lot more.

I scramble from the bed and go hurtling downstairs. Dad's in the kitchen talking on his Bluetooth, something about chasing down the crooks from Accounts. I pounce on him and wrap my arms tight around him. "I'll play along." I laugh. "I'll pretend I'm mad that all you got me was Tic Tacs. But I know. I get it. And I can't wait." Dad looks down at me like I'm a candy wrapper a strong wind has whipped into his face. He mumbles, "I'll talk to you later" into his headset and then untangles himself from me. He's got this expression that's halfway between surprise and annoyance. He's keeping up the pretense he doesn't know I know. "What's going on, Bridge?" he says. Oh, he's good.

"Nothing much," I shrug, playing along. "I guess I should stop expecting birthdays to be a big thing in this family. I guess I should just be grateful for a few green Tic Tacs." He starts to pull off his jacket. Then he stops and looks at me. He looks at me exactly like Joanna did this morning. Except he doesn't hide his surprise. His eyes widen. He turns to the calendar stuck on the fridge door. When he turns back to face me, his expression is mournful. "Oh, Bridget," he sighs.

"I'm so sorry." He slumps down heavily on a stool. "Get it together," he says to himself, almost under his breath but just loud enough for me to hear. He shakes his head sorrowfully. "I've got no excuses, Bridge. I would have hated it if this had happened to me when I was your age. But I promise I'll make it up to you. Where do you wanna go? What do you wanna do? Pick a place to eat and a movie you want to see. Call Joanna, see if she wants to come with. Then we'll go into the office and get you a gift card. A sixty-dollar one. And again, I'm sorry."

Dad gives me a consoling hug and a kiss on the forehead. He leaves the kitchen and, as he heads upstairs, I hear him talking on his Bluetooth. "We are officially the worst parents in the world. We forgot Bridget's birthday. We're taking her out tonight. Buy her something on your way home. Like balloons or a unicorn or something."

His voice fades away. Now I'm confused. He's not playing one of his pranks. He forgot my birthday for real. They all did. So where did that bag come from?

CHAPTER FOUR

Whole New You

It doesn't come up. The subject of the brown-and-pink-striped bag and the contents therein does not come up. It does not come up because I do not bring it up. It also does not come up because we do not go out as a family-plus-Joanna to the street dance sequel I have picked for us to see. We do not go out after the movie as a family-plus-Joanna to dinner at my favorite restaurant, Leatherby's Family Creamery. We got ready to go out as a family-plus-Joanna but then Mom received a last-minute call from her head office that there was a van filled with wigs that should have been delivered to a wig store but was still in the depot and the wig-store owner was furious. "Flipping his wig," I cracked, but no one was listening. Mom had to go and put out that fire. She promised to join us as soon as the wig crisis was over. Ryan didn't show. No message. No excuses. So it was just me, Dad, Natalie, and Joanna.

Dad slept through the movie. Joanna ate three bags of popcorn and then spent the duration of the movie picking kernels out of her teeth. Natalie tried to turn off her phone out of courtesy to other moviegoers but texts from her many, many friends kept flooding in and she felt it would be rude to ignore them. Dad didn't turn his phone off, either. It woke him twenty minutes before the climactic dance-off, which I never got to see because the call was from Ryan. We had to pick him up from the police station. (He had nothing to do with throwing eggs at a bus filled with nuns. It was the people he was with. *Right.*) The evening ended with me sitting in the back of the Jeep Compass squished between Natalie and Ryan, who was talking about his regular visits to the holding cell in Reindeer Crescent's police precinct.

"You're taking a man's freedom away, that's a tough pill to swallow," reflected Ryan of his forty-seven minutes of incarceration. "But they're just walls, walls and bars. They can't cage the kid's soul."

Natalie stopped replying to the newest batch of texts. "I'm going to start writing to prisoners," she announced.

"You're not," said Dad.

"They need to know someone cares," she said.

"What if you started writing to a serial killer who likes wearing little girls' skins?" Ryan laughed. "What if you invited him over for Thanksgiving?"

"He's not coming for Thanksgiving," said Dad. "We've already got Grandma Jean to deal with."

"I'm going to write to prisoners, I don't care what you think," said Natalie. "Everyone needs to know there's someone out there who's listening to them."

"Thanks for coming out for my birthday," I said.

Ryan kept laughing at Natalie, who kept arguing with him and Dad. Joanna kept digging for buried kernels. I don't think anybody heard me.

Meanwhile, no one took responsibility for the birthday bag. Outside my immediate family, my prime suspect was Joanna. She's never said or done anything nice for anyone. Not even me and I'm her best-slash-only friend. But what if she had hidden depths? What if there was a sweet, nice, warm, generous person hiding deep inside her, desperate to come out but scared of how she'd be received? So, a couple of days after the Birthday That

Never Was, while we were walking to school, I waited for Joanna to take a breath between *I-hate*s and tentatively asked the question.

"Did you . . . leave something outside my front door?"

Joanna responded with one of her *What are you, a moron?* squints. "Yeah," she replied, oozing fake sincerity. "I left a baby in a box. I want the Wilders to bring it up as their own. 'Cause they did such a stellar job with you."

I returned her squint with a stare of disbelief. Splotches of red appeared on Joanna's face, indicating she was aware she went a step too far. "I mean . . . ," she started to say. "I wasn't . . ."

I let her flounder for a moment. "So that's a no," I finally said.

After I crossed Joanna off the list, I was left with distant family members. Uncle Leo and Aunt Anne. Doubtful. They still owe Mom and Dad money. Buying me presents instead of paying back the loan would trigger a huge family rift. Of course, there is another option. It could be one of my bio-parents. I mean, wouldn't that make sense? The bag was dumped anonymously on the doorstep. It's a gesture but an impersonal one. Thing is, if I go down that road then I have to think about talking to Mom and Dad about the contents of the bag. Which means a discussion about whether I'm ready to meet the people who gave me away. And the contents of the bag suggest that whoever packed it does not know me at all. So I bury that option.

I let four days of *maybes* and *what-ifs* go by. More and more, I feel like the victim of a cruel prank. What did I end up with? A phone that doesn't work. Lip balm I can't open. Glasses I can't see with. Tic Tacs I've no interest in sucking. And keys. Useless keys. Oh yeah, and the invite to the sale that's probably a fake. But who would want to mess with me like this? And then it hits me. Brendan Chew. Of course. Obviously. If he gets laughs with Midget Wilder, what's he going to get with this goody-bag prank? But how far would he really go to embarrass me? I sit down at the computer and Google search IMAGE UNLTD's Reindeer Crescent store. It has a very fancy-looking site with music and videos and pictures of crazy-expensive dresses and tops. *Brendan Chew put in a lot of work to make me look stupid*, I think. I call the number on the site. "Hello, Image Unlimited, how may I help you?" breathes a female voice on the other end. I hang up. Weird. It's a real store. Or it's an incredibly complex prank. Either way, I need answers.

I hop off the bus at Reindeer Crescent's single-story mall and walk inside the shopping center with as much confidence as I can muster. I see midafternoon shoppers milling around the Gap. Women come out of the brow-shaping salon. A boy and girl walk hand-in-hand into the Pretzel Choice. What I don't see is IMAGE UNLTD.

Then I spot it. Nestling between Aéropostale and Forever 21. The one shop in the mall that's not trying to draw attention to itself. The window is all black except for the silver letters I and U. I can already tell this is not the kind of place where I'll feel comfortable. (I tend to like shops that *are* drawing attention to themselves.) But I've come this far. So I walk up to the tinted-black door and give it a push. Bright white light spills out. I take another cautious step inside. The whiteness seems to stretch out forever. The walls, the floor, the ceiling. There are clothes on display and a few other customers. But the whiteness swallows everything else up. I feel like I'm in heaven. That feeling does not go away as a girl wafts toward me. A very tall girl. A very tall, very, very beautiful girl who might be in her late teens or early twenties and who is smiling at me like I'm a long-lost relative.

"Hi," she says, sounding genuinely excited. "I'm Xan. With an X." I would have replied that I'm Bridget with a B but strangely, right at this particular second, I can't seem to remember my name. It's a combination of the whiteness and the Xan. Instead, I brandish the invitation that has been folded over many times and still bears the clammy warmth of being clutched in my hand. Xan with an X takes the invitation, glances at it, and then smiles at me. The light radiating from her insane veneers suddenly makes the rest of the store look like the inside of an old shoe. "Oh my God, Bridget," she says. "I've got something that is so right for you. It'll change your life. Do you trust me?"

I want to say *Trust you? I don't even know you*, but once again, close proximity to Xan with an X seems to have robbed me of my power of speech. She slips an arm through mine and guides me across the whiteness. As I trot alongside, taking three steps to her one, she plucks items from the white walls. The deep red of her long sharp fingernails stands out in stark contrast to the surrounding whiteness. I follow her to the far end of the store, where she points me to a changing room. "Let me know when you're ready," Xan says, handing me the clothes she's picked out. "I can't wait to see how these look on you."

"Um . . . I'm not sure I can afford all this," I say as the door begins to close.

"It's a special promotion," Xan replies. "And you're a special customer."

No one's ever called me special before. At least not in the positive way she's saying it.

"So does that mean it's . . ."

"Our gift to you."

And then I'm alone in the spacious white changing room. That's when I see the outfit Xan with an X thinks is so me. It's a black tracksuit. Black with gold stripes. Much like the ones I wear seven days out of any given week. I'm disappointed. It's not that I really believed Xan had seen me through different eyes or that she was going to remake me in her own blindingly beautiful image. (Except I did. That's exactly what I believed. I don't need Brendan Chew to make me feel stupid. Not when I'm so good at it.) *Shut up*, I tell myself. *You got a free tracksuit.* There's a knock on the door. It opens a crack. "My eyes are closed," Xan singsongs. "I just wanted you to try these on. They're so you. If you like them, consider them part of the gift." Xan slides a shoe box into the changing room. I open it. Sneakers. Black-and-gold-striped sneakers. Much like the ones I wear seven days out of every given week. *Shut up*, I tell myself. *Free sneakers.*

"If you need any help I'm right out here," Xan calls.

"I'm fine," I mutter.

"I can't wait to see you. I'm so, so excited!"

Now, I know it's Xan with an X's job to say things like that and, years from now, I can totally imagine Natalie working in a place like this and saying the exact same sort of thing, but it's been a long time since anyone said they were excited to see me.

So I change into my new black-and-gold tracksuit. It feels *fantastic*, warm and luxurious. I get actual tingles running up and down my arms and legs as I put it on. Zipping the jacket, I get the strangest sensation, as if the whole suit is *molding* itself to my body. Which is to say, it feels *nothing* like the slobby suits I generally slob around in. I squeeze out of my old beat-up Pumas and into the fresh pair. I feel like I'm walking on a cloud. I look at myself in the changing room mirror. Ordinary-looking girl. Five foot four. Little on the pale side. Dark eyes, almost black. Due a haircut. You could park an SUV in the gap between her teeth. But black and gold might be her colors. That girl in the mirror is smiling.

"Knock knock," sings out Xan.

I open the changing room door. Xan's smile almost gives me sunstroke.

"Oh, Bridget," she breathes. "You look so . . ." She can't complete the sentence. She flaps her hands at her eyes.

"That bad, huh?" I joke. But even though I know

she's exaggerating for effect, I feel like I look okay.

"Don't change," she says. "Wear them home. Get used to them. Get used to the new you."

As with every other command she's given me during my time in IMAGE UNLTD, I do exactly what she says.

CHAPTER FIVE

The Young Gazelle

As I walk away from the mall and head toward the bus stop, I look at my black-and-gold-clad self in every store window I pass. I like what I see. I like it so much I wish there was someone here to confirm that I look as good as I think I do. And then there's Dale Tookey! Literally at the exact moment I thought that, he came skittering out of a doughnut store a few yards away from me, clutching a paper bag. Things are turning around for Bridget Wilder. *Should I act like I don't see him?* Because that's worked so well for me in the past. *No. Not this time.* Not this so-called Midget. I smile straight at him. That's right, Dale Tookey, this black-and-gold girl is smiling back at you. So what are you gonna do? Are you gonna step up or are you . . . ?

No! He's turning away! He's looking over his shoulder. Like he's deliberately trying to ignore me.

And now he's running straight past me! Without even looking in my direction. I stare after him, stunned.

I'm so stupid! I *knew* he never smiled at me. But I'm at my least grotesque ever right now. Why would he run right past me? What would make him do that?

"Doom Patrol!"

I whip around and see why Dale ran. The four guys who hassled him outside the fro-yo place are hot on his trail. For a second, I'm happy and relieved. It wasn't *me* he was running from. Then I remember his face after the Doom Patrol got through with him. I don't want him to suffer through that again. But, by the evil grins on the stubbly faces of the four thugs who charge past me, I've got a sinking feeling they've singled him out for special attention. They're not putting any effort in their pursuit, either. They're not running. Just shadowing him, staying close enough to intimidate him with their continued presence so they can extract maximum amusement from his misery. They're doing that "Doom Patrol!" chant over and over, getting louder and louder. I need to do something this time. But what? I take a hesitant step in their direction and . . .

I'm running!

I mean, *I'm* not running. But I am. It's like I'm not in control. I look down and my legs are flying with the speed and grace of a young gazelle. (Young Gazelle could be my alter-ego name!) My black-and-gold sneakers are moving so fast they're a blur beneath me. My arms slice back and forward, propelling me ever faster. I don't know what's happening. It's like I'm in the passenger seat of a car and I don't know who's driving. I just know they like to go really, *really* fast. Within seconds, I'm bearing down on a Doom Patrol member. Something's happening. I'm on the balls of my feet. My hips start to sink toward the ground. And then . . . I jump!

I've gone out of my way to never be in a position where I have to do things like jump in front of people. But no one's told whatever has control of me because my feet have definitely left the ground.

Two things happen as I soar through the air.

1. I make a noise that sounds like *Eeeeeeee*.
2. I land smoothly and accurately with one foot on either shoulder of the shortest Doom Patrol member.

I gasp for breath but the *Eeeee* continues. It's not me. It's the boy beneath my black-and-gold sneakers. He's screaming in shock and fear. I feel him sway beneath me. His knees start to buckle.

"Sorry," I start to say. Then it's *Eeeee* again and this time it's definitely me because I feel my hips sinking. Just as the Doom Patrol dude crumples, whimpering, to the ground, I shoot off his shoulders and . . . *Eeeee . . . I somersault straight over the heads of the other three.*

I'm now midway through a three-hundred-and-sixty degree flip and, as I rotate through the air, I think, *I am the girl who doesn't get picked for teams. I stay on the bench. I've used the same please-excuse-Bridget-from-gym-class note for eight months. The gym teacher always looks at it like it's the first time she's ever seen it. Or me.*

And yet . . .

I land perfectly in front of the three Doom Patrol guys. *Wow, they're ugly,* I think. *Wow, they're big. Wow, my stomach is churning.* One of them is wearing dark glasses. I sneak a peek at my reflection. As I feared. Hair wild. Face scarlet. Glasses all over the place. So much for my big moment of looking good. While I'm checking myself out in the guy's lenses, I see Dale standing behind me. The three Doom Guys recover from their surprise. They go to shove past me but I stop them. When I say *I* stop them, that is not accurate. My arms spread. I do not spread them. The Doom Guys start laughing.

"Your bodyguard's a beast," one of them jeers over my shoulder.

"How much you pay her?" mocks another.

"I don't even know her," I hear Dale shout back. Not really what I want to hear.

The three Doom Guys stop laughing and give me cold hard stares designed to strike fear into my heart. It works.

"Move. Now," one of them growls.

I move. Or rather my foot does. My right foot. It spins me halfway around and then yanks me back and as I'm being yanked back, it does this wide, sweeping one-hundred-and-eighty-degree kick. The three Doom Guys rear back. They look at me in shock. Then they look at the ground. Where their baseball hats sit faceup. Yep, *please excuse Bridget Wilder from gym class* just flew through the air. Again.

The most vocal Doom Guy fixes me with his meanest stare. "You don't want to get into this with us, little girl," he says.

"You're right," I agree. "I don't."

"I don't even know her," repeats Dale Tookey from behind me.

"You know a few cute tricks," growls the lead Doom Guy. "But you push us one more time and we push back. You won't be so cute once we're done with you."

I'm tempted to thank the Doom Guy for calling me cute but my arms have other ideas. They have decided to spread out again. My right knee raises in the air, higher than I'm comfortable with. I feel like I'm going to topple over. But I don't. My right foot extends slightly. It circles the air. The three Doom Guys stare at my right foot like it's a snake waiting to strike. *Wait, is this my fighting stance? I've seen enough of Ryan's rip-their-heads-off video games to recognize an unbeatable fighting stance and apparently this is mine. I might call it Gazelle Stance.* The Doom Guys try to maintain their mean, intimidating looks but they also begin to back away. Slowly. One inch at a time. They point threatening fingers both directly at me and over my shoulder. Forced into a humiliating retreat by the Young Gazelle.

Once they've gone, I turn around to face Dale Tookey.

"You dropped your doughnuts" is the first thing I say. It's true. His paper bag is on the ground by his feet.

"I don't even know . . . ," he begins to say.

"You do so," I snap back at him. It's like he'd rather have been beaten to a bloody pulp than admit knowing me. "You might not know my name. But you've seen me. We have a bunch of classes together. You've seen me hundreds of times. You smiled at me."

That last bit slipped out by accident.

He looks annoyed. At *me*! "Well," he says, "I didn't ask you to do that. I didn't ask you to help me."

Of all the unbelievable things that just happened, this boy's ingratitude is maybe the most unbelievable.

"It'll never happen again," I assure him.

"I don't care," he says.

He starts to walk away.

"You're just going to leave your doughnuts lying there?" I call after him.

"You have them," he shouts back, not even looking around.

I'm not eating doughnuts after they've been on the ground, even if they are still in the bag. I don't want to leave them lying there littering the sidewalk. But why should I pick up after that ungrateful jerkface? And why am I thinking about Dale Tookey's doughnuts when I just ran, jumped, flipped, kicked, balanced on one foot, and debuted my lethal fighting stance. Six things I've never done before. Six things I'm pretty sure I *didn't* do on my own. And now I'm freaking out. I feel my face burning. My heart is pounding. I don't know what's happening to me. I start to walk back to the mall. I need to be close to the calming influence of Xan with an X. She'll make me feel better. But I'm not going back to the mall. At least, my black-and-gold sneakers aren't. They spin me around. They start moving, faster and faster. My legs start pumping. My elbows slice the air.

I'm running again!

CHAPTER SIX

Spool

O h my God, am I gonna kick the front door down?
No. I slow down as I head up the driveway to
my house. I'm gasping for breath and soaked in sweat.
I spit out something solid but squishy—*was that a fly?*
Ewww, I think it might have been a fly! Then I reach for
my keys and, with shaking hands, make a few attempts
to open the door. What do I tell my family? *Mom! Dad!*
Guess what? I've lost all control of my limbs. Quick, throw a
net over me.

I don't have to worry. No one's home. I need a giant
glass of milk right now to calm me down. But I'm not

going to get it. My sneakers walk me to the stairs. They sprint me up the steps and hurry me into my bedroom. *Where a phone is ringing.*

I don't recognize the ringtone. It's some kind of bleepy-bloopy electro thing. Not my ancient Nokia. I look around the room for the source of the sound. *The bag!* The bleeping noise is coming from the brown-and-pink bag I consigned to my closet with all the other junk I refuse to let Mom toss but will never find any use for. I pull open the door. The ringtone is louder and clearer. I shove a hand deep into the gift bag and pull out the phone. The unactivated iPhone without a charger. It keeps bleeping and blooping, but I still don't see any buttons to press or any icons on the all-black screen. Suddenly the all-black vanishes and a face fills the screen. A man's face. Well, I say a man. It looks more like a baby's face. Round, pink, chubby, and hairless.

"Spool," the baby-faced man suddenly says.

"Aah!" I squeal and drop the phone.

"Hello? Hello?" says the voice.

I pick the phone back up and stare at the screen.

"Spool," the face repeats. "Brian Spool. I work with your father."

"At Pottery Barn?"

"No," says Brian Spool. "Not that father."

"Is there another one I don't know about?" I say automatically. Then, "Oh." And I stop talking.

Brian Spool blinks at me. A thumb appears at the bottom of the screen. The thumb rubs Brian Spool's chin for a moment. When he finally looks back at me, he seems uncomfortable.

"There's no easy way to tell you this . . ." He's not telling me anything! His eyes are darting from side to side and he's rubbing his chin again.

"Tell me what?" I say.

"This isn't in my job description," sighs Spool. "I'm not good at this kind of thing. I thought it would be easy if I just came right out and told you but now I'm thinking I should have written something down. At least a cheat sheet."

I've had enough. "Tell Brendan Chew I said hi." I drop the phone back in the bag and start to close my closet door.

"Who?" says Spool.

His voice does not come from inside the bag. It comes from somewhere else. I turn my head slowly.

Spool's pink hairless face fills my computer screen. Which I put to sleep before I left for school this morning. Unless I didn't. But even if I didn't, I still couldn't explain what Spool's face is doing there.

"How are you doing this?" I ask, trying not to betray how uneasy I suddenly feel.

"I have a satellite," he says.

"So do we."

"Not a satellite dish. An actual satellite. In space. Like a lot of secret counterintelligence agencies do. Only ours is better."

I'm not sure how to react. I don't know what to believe.

"Go to the window," Spool tells me. "Look to your right."

"Don't tell me what to do," I mutter.

"Just do it," he sighs. "It'll be worth it."

I shuffle over to the window, and I look right. I can just about see Mrs. Telk, the old, old, *old* neighbor lady who accused Ryan of kidnapping her cat. (He claims she sat on it by mistake. Jury's out.) Mrs. Telk is waiting for the WALK signal so she can teeter and ache her way across the road. The signal turns green. She begins her slow voyage. The light turns red again. It wasn't green for even a second. Telk staggers backward. The light says WALK again. Telk shudders forward.

DON'T WALK. She looks confused and even more shaky than usual. I hear a high-pitched snicker. "That's me," laughs Spool. "I'm doing that. With my satellite."

"Stop," I say. "She's old. She could fall."

"If that happened, I could have a crew of paramedics attending to her within seconds. That's the kind of technology I have at my fingertips."

I watch Telk finally make it across the road without interruptions. In fact, the WALK sign seems to glow green a few seconds longer than usual, changing only when she's safely on the sidewalk.

"Good for you," I say. "What's that got to do with me?"

Spool coughs into his hand. He takes a deep breath. "Like I said, I work with your father. At Section 23."

"What's Section 23?"

"It's not a secret, extremely classified department of the CIA whose highly trained operatives are only called into action when the safety of the world is threatened by enemies so powerful and unstoppable there is no one else capable of doing the job."

I stare at Spool's pink face. He looks deadly serious. Like a deadly serious baby.

"Then what is it?" I ask.

"What's what?"

"Section . . . what you just said . . ."

"I didn't say anything."

And I thought Dale Tookey was annoying.

"Yes, you did. I heard you. You said . . ."

"I *denied* the existence of a covert unit of highly trained agents headed by Carter Strike."

"Who?"

"Nobody. Not a man hated and feared by enemies of freedom. Not the finest and most selfless man it's ever been my privilege to work with. Not your father."

"I'm hanging up, Spool."

He looks pained. "I'm trained to deny everything when interacting with a civilian. But I guess you're not exactly . . . okay, remember when I said the words *not your father*?"

I nod. "I was here when it happened."

"That was not entirely accurate. The intel I am about to share with you is strictly classified."

No one's ever shared classified intel with me before. I wait for the oddball on my screen to continue.

"Thirteen years, nine months, two weeks, and an unknown number of hours ago, Special Agent Strike and an unknown female embarked on what was to be a short but passionate relationship . . ."

I'm already hoping Spool's about done with the classified intel. I need to take a shower. I'm all sweaty and gross from the running.

"The world was then as it is now: in crisis. Special

Agent Strike had a job to do. A job that required him to change identities and go into deep cover, where he could pass unnoticed among the enemies of freedom. A job where he couldn't be reached so he didn't know the unknown female had given birth to a child . . ."

"Spool," I interrupt. "I'm really hungry."

"A child who was given up for adoption a matter of minutes after her birth."

I stop thinking about my shower and my dinner.

"Why are you telling me this?"

"Why do you think I'm telling you this?" asks Spool.

"Don't answer a question with a question."

Spool looks at me with sympathy. "He didn't know. Not until very recently. Agent Strike's reaction was similar to yours."

Suddenly I'm finding it hard to breathe. I slump down on to the floor. I try to speak but nothing comes out.

"I don't understand," I manage to whisper.

"I'm sorry to be the one to have to break it to you like this, Bridget. Your real father is Special Agent Carter Strike."

I say nothing.

Spool's face vanishes. The screen is filled with a copy of an official-looking form. An adoption form. Signed by Jeff and Nancy Wilder. The image is replaced by a picture of man who looks like a movie star. Dark hair. Pale skin. Dark eyes, almost black. A gap between his teeth.

The man's handsome face disappears to be replaced by Spool's face. Which does not look good by comparison.

"That guy could be anyone," I say.

"I'm not lying to you," he says. "I have no reason to."

"You could be pulling a prank. A huge prank."

"The CIA doesn't pull pranks. Not even its most secret departments."

"That guy is my father? My real actual father?"

"He is," says Spool.

"And my mother?" I croak. "Who is she?"

"Untraceable at this time," says Spool.

A pink-faced man has just told me my real parents are a secret agent and a woman who doesn't exist.

I think my head is about to explode.

CHAPTER SEVEN

Bond

"**B**ridget, listen . . ."

Oh my God. OH MY GOD! This is bigger than the throne of Luxembourg. THIS IS BIGGER THAN STEPHEN COLBERT!

"Bridget, this is important . . ."

Do Mom and Dad know? Are they spies, too? Maybe Pottery Barn's a cover!

"Bridget!" yells Spool from the screen. I'd forgotten he was there.

What if Ryan's a counterspy? What if Natalie's *one?*

"Bridget!" Spool shouts. "I understand this is hard

for you. You should probably talk to a qualified professional who can help you deal with what I've told you.
Unfortunately, you can't. Because the conversations
taking place in this room are secret and highly confi-
dential."

"Do my family, my real family, know about this?" I
ask.

Spool shakes his head no.

"Can I tell them?"

That head shake again.

"I'm expected to keep something this huge a secret?"
I'm about to protest but then I don't. I don't protest
because it hits me that I just used the words *huge* and
secret in a sentence about me. I've never had a huge secret
before. It feels good.

"Bridget," Spool keeps shouting. "Can you pay attention for a second?"

"Sorry," I say. "I'm all yours."

"There's a reason we made contact in this particular
manner. If you watch the screen, you'll understand."

Spool's face vanishes. Another face fills the screen.
The handsome man. The man with the dark eyes and the
gap between his teeth.

"Hi, Bridget," the man says. And now I'm con-
centrating on my computer screen. The man's head is

slightly lowered. He looks up at me, nods like he's a tiny bit embarrassed.

I whisper back, "Hi."

"This isn't how I wanted us to meet," he says.

"Me neither," I start to say. "This is such a surpr—"

"You deserve more from me than a recorded message."

Oh. I'm not really talking to him. Whoever he is.

"I'd rather see you face-to-face. But you've talked to Spool. You know the kind of life I lead. I don't always get to do the things I want to do. So this is the best I can do right now. I know this is a lot to deal with. But I've read Spool's profile on you. I know you're strong and I know you're smart and capable. In fact, the more I read about you, the more I thought, This is the kind of person I would recruit."

"Recruit for what?" I say. And then I remember he can't hear or see me.

"For Section 23," he says. "Which sounds crazy. Because you're a kid. But I was seventeen when they recruited me, and you're a lot more together than I was at your age."

"Dude, you *really* don't know me," I say. But I'm flattered.

"So I said to Spool, what if we brought Bridget on

board as an undercover junior operative? Assigned her Reindeer Crescent Middle School and the surrounding neighborhood. Put her in charge of identifying, profiling, and surveilling individuals with the potential to become future security problems. Gave her the tools to do the job. A little like the precrime department in that Tom Cruise movie *Minority Report*."

"I like movies where there's dancing," I tell the screen. "Where there's a big dance-off at the end."

The recorded version of Carter Strike goes on. "Obviously, Spool looked at me like I was nuts. But that's our deal. He looks at me like I'm nuts. Then I save the world. So now Spool's come around to my way of thinking."

I listen to Special Agent Carter Strike's calm, persuasive voice and I imagine most people come around to his way of thinking.

"But this isn't about what Spool thinks. I'm going be honest with you, Bridget. I'm scared."

He stares at me from the computer screen.

"Of what?" I say.

"I can disable a nuclear warhead. I can topple an enemy government. I know three ways to eliminate an adversary using only a Styrofoam cup. But I don't know how to be a dad."

You're talking to me, I think. *You're acknowledging I exist. That's a start.*

"I want to try, though," he goes on. "That's why I thought, if you knew a little of what my life is like . . . not the nuclear warhead part or the killing with cups. Just a taste of the spying part . . . there wouldn't be such a distance between us. There would be a bond."

I know he can't see me but Carter Strike is looking right at me. And he looks like he wants that bond more than anything.

"I do, too," I tell him, even though I know he can't hear me. "Want it. The bond."

"I wish I could talk longer. We will. Soon. But, for now, think about what I said. I can't wait to meet you. Bye, Bridget."

The screen goes black.

Then it goes pink.

"So?" says Spool.

I don't reply. This is way too much to take in. My real father is a secret agent. Who wants *me* to be a secret agent.

"You want to do it," Spool says. "I've got a sense about you."

"I've got a sense you're a moron," I tell him. "Do you know anything about me?"

"I know you can take care of yourself in the face of conflict. Like you did this afternoon."

This afternoon seems like ten million years ago.

"The tracksuit," Spool reminds me. "Your speed, your balance, your martial-arts skills. I did that."

"What do you mean, you did that?"

For the first time, Spool smiles. He looks like a baby who's just enjoyed a loud and satisfying burp.

"This was actually kind of brilliant. I took a random sample of surveillance tapes of your father's physical confrontations and created an algorithm that . . ."

"Spool!" I snap. "You're losing me."

"Sorry," he says, and he looks disappointed he's not getting the opportunity to explain his brilliant idea in lengthy and mind-numbing detail.

"The tracksuit and the sneakers have been designed to anticipate potential conflict in any given situation and react to it like your father would."

"Shut up," I retort.

"You shut up," he says, sounding offended. "It works. You saw it work. You were there."

"Sorry," I say. "I didn't mean *shut up* shut up. I meant . . . I'm *wearing* my dad? Is that what you're telling me?"

"Well," he says. "The suit was created using nano-technology, which, at its core . . ."

"Spool!"

"Yes, essentially, you're wearing garments that exactly imitate Special Agent Strike's skill set. Put in the most simplistic terms . . ."

"I love the most simplistic terms."

"While you're wearing the suit and the shoes, you can run like him and fight like him."

The stuff that happened this afternoon immediately comes rushing back to me. Oh my God! I jumped onto that Doom Patrol kid's shoulders! And I hate heights. I flipped right over the other dudes. I kicked their caps off. I intimidated them with my unnamed fighting stance. But, wait . . .

"I got the suit and the shoes from a . . ."

Spool is smiling a little too smugly for my liking. "A Section 23 base entirely staffed by our operatives," he says, talking over me.

"So the tall girl who served me was . . ."

"Section 23."

"But what if I hadn't wanted a tracksuit and sneakers? What if I'd wanted a dress or a scarf or . . ."

"Then my research would have been wrong. And that's never happened."

Me? A secret agent? Insane. But my dad thinks I can do it and he saves the world on a regular basis. And I want to get to know my dad. I want there to be a bond as much as he does. I think I'm actually seriously considering becoming a spy. Spies are secretive, right? They lurk in the shadows. They blend into the background. No one notices them. They're more or less invisible. *I'm perfect spy material!*

A few minutes ago I thought I was about to have a panic attack. A minute ago I thought I was about to throw up. And now? I'm laughing. Talk about an emotional roller coaster!

"Is everything okay?" asks Spool.

"Yeah." I grin. "I just . . . I don't even know how to deal with this."

"Maybe you want to take a break before we go into the rest of the plan."

I feel my eyes go big. "There's more?"

"There's a whole bagful," says Spool.

CHAPTER EIGHT

Toy Story

I've upended the contents of the brown-and-pink bag on top of my bed. I hold the box of green Tic Tacs up to the computer screen.

"Cameras," says Spool.

I take a single Tic Tac from the box, hold it in my hand, and stare at it. Looks green and normal to me. I pop it in my mouth.

"That's hundreds of thousands of dollars' worth of equipment you've got in your mouth," shouts Spool.

"All that money didn't help the taste," I say.

"Touch the screen of the phone," says Spool.

I roll the Tic Tac around my mouth, lean forward, and tap my middle finger on the phone. Spool's face vanishes again. All I see is . . . it's blurry . . . I see pink and white and something metallic and a flash of green and . . . oh my God, I'm looking at the inside of my mouth! It's horrific. I spit the Tic Tac into my hand and stare at it. I look over at the phone and the screen is showing a close-up of my face. It's even more horrific. I toss the tiny candy camera across the room.

"Hundreds of thousands of dollars," moans Spool. "Years of research. Not meant to be sucked."

"Why make it look like a Tic Tac, then?" As I ask the question, I know the answer. Because you can hide a piece of candy anywhere and nobody will notice it. Ooh, I can put one in Ryan's bedroom. Find out what's *really* going on with him. I can put one in Dale Tookey's pocket. Not that I'd want to. But I could.

"The phone is bulletproof, fireproof, and missile-proof," Spool says.

"Is there a chance someone's going to fire a missile at me?"

"There's always a chance," he says. "It can disguise your voice, translate up to one hundred and thirty-five foreign languages, and act as a handy flashlight."

I throw my old cell phone in the trash. I just upgraded.

"The secret agent apple didn't fall too far from the tree," says Spool. "You're turning into a spy right in front of me."

"I never said a word," I protest.

"You didn't have to," he smirks. "It's written all over your face."

"What about these?" I say, holding up the thick black glasses. "Can I see through walls?"

"No, but you can see through lies."

"Shut up!" I gasp. "Seriously?"

I yank my glasses off and put the black pair on. I blink a few times. What was once blurry is now crystal clear. Technology!

"Look at me," says Spool. "Get close."

Not a fun assignment, but I hold the phone inches from my face.

"I much prefer dealing with you to my regular work," he says.

As he speaks, green-tinged data floats in front of my eyes. The words **forced smile** hover by Spool's face.

Body temperature elevated. Perspiration detected. Eye movement to the right. Vocal pitch rising.

"You like your regular work more than dealing with me?" I snap. "What's wrong with me?"

"I was demonstrating how the technology works," says Spool.

Throat lubrication detected.

I pull the glasses off. "Too weird," I say. "How can I ever trust anyone again?" Spool nods sadly. "It comes with being a spy. The short answer is, you can't."

I put the glasses back on. *What's left?* I pull the USB drive out of the bag.

"What's this?"

"It's a superfast data storage device with infinite capacity."

"Wow," I say, hoping my *wow* communicates the depth of my disinterest. I pick up the keys and jangle them in front of the phone, hoping that communicates the depth of my interest. My very interested interest.

"A car, right?" I ask. "My spy car."

Spool nods. "Yes."

"Yeah, right." I grin.

My lie-detecting glasses say . . . *nothing.* They say nothing. Spool's not lying. He's truthing!

"Shut up! I get a car? My own car? What kind is it?" I know nothing about cars so it doesn't matter what he says.

"The car is for emergency situations that will never arise. But if they do, the car will take care of everything."

"Will it take care of me not being able to drive and also being thirteen?"

"Yes," says Spool.

I don't know what this means but . . . *I already love the car.*

Spool says, "Tonight before I go to sleep, I will drop to my knees and pray that you never experience any kind of emergency."

Once again, my glasses are free of lie-detecting data. But I find the mental picture of Spool on his knees praying for my continued well-being sort of touching. Embarrassing but touching. There's one last item on the bed. The yellow tube of pear-flavored lip balm.

"This is the most important thing I'm going to tell you today," intones Spool. "Never put the lip balm anywhere near your lips. Or your face. Point it away from you at all times."

"Why?"

"Face it away from you and twist the bottom."

I turn the bottom of the tube with my thumb and forefinger. The top pops off.

"Point it at something that is of no value to you."

Everything in my bedroom is of value to me. My

books. My clothes. My computer. My movie posters. My photographs. Even the stuff in my closet that's been piling up for years and I'll never get rid of. I hop off the bed and open the closet door. Empty boxes, single sneakers long divorced from their pairs, Billy the Singing Bass, too-small T-shirts, broken tennis rackets, and on and on and on . . .

I point the lip balm at the clutter.

"Now give the tube a single squeeze."

I follow Spool's instructions. I tighten my finger around the lip balm and . . . a flash of razor-thin white light comes out of the top. It's a light saber! My lip balm tube is a light saber. I aim the white light at a single sneaker. It disappears. In its place is a small pile of ashes. I laugh out loud. I point the lip balm again.

The empty boxes. Ashes. The T-shirts. Ashes. Billy the Singing Bass. Ashes.

I spin around and scream "Oh my God!" at the phone. The light from the lip balm tube turns one of my desk legs to ashes. My computer and everything else on the desk slides onto the floor.

"Squeeze the tube again!" yells Spool. I do. The light vanishes. The top pops back on.

"It's a laser," explains Spool. "Use it sparingly and carefully. You might also want to make a note of its additional components. Two squeezes activates the Taser function. Three, the smoke machine."

I have no words. I just gasp, stare, and nod. I look over at my desk with its missing leg. I could probably have propped it up with my tennis racket, if I hadn't also reduced that to ashes *with my lip balm laser.*

"All right," says Spool. "I think you've got enough to deal with for one day. You can contact me via the phone and I you. We'll discuss your first assignment in due course."

"Wait!" I yell at the screen. Spool stares back at me.

"Spool, what's he like? My dad. I mean, you and him are friends, right?"

The screen on my phone goes black.

"What's all that stuff on your bed?" says my mom.

I let out a gasp and feel myself flinch. I didn't hear her walk in.

"You didn't even knock! Don't just walk in without knocking."

I'm freaked out by Mom's sudden appearance. It's not a good idea to scare me right now. Not when I'm standing here with a laser in my hand.

She stares at my face.

"What are those? Where did you get them?"

She's peering at my new, thick, black lie-detecting

glasses. Which are not providing me with any telltale data right now.

"In school."

"Someone gave them to you?"

A few days ago I was desperate to have Mom remember my birthday and shower me with attention. Now? Now I've got a huge secret. And I don't want to answer any questions.

"What happened to your desk?" she asks. "All your things are on the ground."

I just want her to go. "Mom, I know. I'm fixing it. Look, I already tidied the closet, like I said I was going to do."

I point at the closet door. Bad move. I should have swept up the piles of ash.

I can see Mom's eyes pinballing from the ash to the stuff on my bed to my glasses to my broken desk. "Can you go, please?" I shout. "I've got stuff to do for school, an important project. You're stopping me from working."

"Bridget," she says, taking a step toward me. "Is there something you're not telling me?"

Ummmm . . .

CHAPTER NINE

Training Wheels

So I told my mom everything. About my real dad. His secret identity. Section 23. My recruitment. The bagful of gadgets. And she totally got it and was completely supportive. *JK!!* J absolutely and positively K to the nth degree. These lips stayed sealed. At home. In school. With Joanna. Bridget Wilder's little—and by little I mean HUUUUGE—secret stays locked up tight. No one sees anything different about me. I'm just That Girl who's friends with That Other Girl and that's the way I like it. But inside it's a different story. Inside me, there's a volcano waiting to erupt. When do I meet Carter Strike?

What will my first mission be? How long before I hear from Spool again? It's been a whole week since he last made contact.

"Miss . . . uh . . . miss . . . uh . . ."

"Call her Midget."

The sheeplike laughter of Room A117 distracts me from my constant monitoring of the Spool-phone. I look up, ignoring Brendan Chew, and focus on . . . what's his name? He introduced himself to us at the start of the class. He scribbled his name on the board. I think it starts with a D? Maybe a B? No, can't remember. Like it matters. He's a substitute, a round, doughy, red-cheeked guy who's sweating his way through a cheap white nylon shirt that's stretched close to bursting. Wow, listen to me. It's like Joanna's rubbed off on me. I'm sure Mr. D-or-B is a perfectly adequate person, but he's just a substitute, whereas I am a fledgling spy eager to take wing and prove my worth. He waddles toward me.

"Miss . . . uh . . . miss . . ."

As he gets closer, D/B has what can only be described as a flustered look on his face. Not a people person? Uncomfortable around kids? Seems like he made a perfect career choice.

"Your phone," he says.

I stare at him. He's not getting his stubby fingers on

my super-sophisticated communications device.

"Could you, uh, not look at it while I'm talking?"

"Oh my God," yelps Brendan Chew. "You just said what we've all been thinking. Someone finally had the guts to stand up to her."

A117 erupts. Casey Breakbush and her coterie of slim, pretty friends with perfect lives have their hands up over their lovely mouths. Joanna dabs a pink tissue to her eyes in an effort to stem the tears of laughter. The sub stands awkwardly in the middle of the room. He doesn't know what to do with his hands. Not sure what level to pitch his voice. And his lack of classroom leadership makes the laughter grow louder.

My phone vibrates.

I glance down.

There's a picture of Spool's pink face.

I jump out of my seat.

"IfeelsickIneedtoseethenurse." I say it that fast and fly out of A117.

"The midget's got a small problem," says Chew seconds before I depart the room. The laughter is still ringing in my ears as I duck into the girls' room.

"Hello," says Spool.

"Is there a job?" I ask.

"How have you been?" he asks.

"Fine," I say. "Are you calling about a mission?"

"We felt, your father and I, that we should give you time to process . . . ," he says.

"Mission!" I snap, a little louder than I intended.

"There's a pre-mission," he says. "Nothing too taxing. It gives us a chance to see what you can do in the field."

"Training wheels, in other words."

"You can choose to look at it that way. Or you could choose to seize this opportunity with both hands and commit to showing your father that his faith in you is not misplaced."

"What's the pre-mission?" I ask.

"We've received credible intel that an enemy agency is about to engage in a game of misdirection."

"Is that a board game?" I say. "Because I'm not great at those. I don't have the attention span."

"A piece of incriminating information is going to be secretly planted on someone in your school. That piece of information may be no bigger in size than a postage stamp, but it will be imprinted with a secret code. If an unauthorized person is in possession of that secret code, that person will look like a traitor to his-slash-her country. The authorities will be informed about this traitor. The individual will be removed from school and subject to lengthy, painful, and humiliating interrogation. Life-ruining interrogation. And while this is happening . . ."

Spool leaves a significant pause.

I take a wild guess. "Aliens attack?"

He shakes his head no. "The real information will be passed on to the real enemy agent based elsewhere in this state. And no one in authority will notice because they'll be too busy congratulating themselves on the traitor they believe they caught."

"Obviously I completely understand the pre-mission," I say. "But let's pretend I don't. Is what you're asking me to sort of do the same as Nola Milligan slipping Brendan Chew a note telling him Casey Breakbush really likes him? Demented, I know, but hear me out. Casey's boyfriend finds out about the note and beats Chew to a pulp, which would be a joy. But while the boyfriend's attention is directed toward Chew, he doesn't notice Casey giving another, this time genuine, note to the boy she really harbors a secret crush on. The Dale Tookey figure. Or whoever. I picked that name at random. . . ."

I feel myself getting flustered. For once, I'm actually waiting for Spool to interrupt me, which, thankfully, he does.

"The scenarios are similar," he says.

Oh my God! I kind of thought I'd be entrusted

with stopping kids from tracking dog poop onto school property, but this is an actual case with intrigue and importance.

"What do you need me to do?" I say.

"Monitor your surroundings. Observe your fellow students and your teachers. Think like the enemy. Who would you choose if you had to pick someone to frame as a traitor?"

Where do I even start? My mind is reeling with possibilities.

"Is this going to be too much for you?" Spool asks. "We can find you something less demanding."

"This is the exact correct level of demanding," I reply.

"So you're in?"

I'm actually physically tingling with excitement. "I'm in!" I shriek. "I'm all the way in!" My voice echoes around the bathroom. I try to control myself but this is a colossal deal.

"Calm down," he says. "For you to be an effective operative, it's important you do not draw attention to yourself."

"Dude, I've been working on that for the past thirteen years."

"Good," he replies, missing my biting sarcasm. "Stay focused, blend in, and keep a close eye on everyone around you. You'll soon start to notice if people begin to deviate from normal modes of behavior."

"And if they do, I take them down with maximum force," I say.

"It's not a takedown," he says, immediately sucking the fun out of the pre-mission. "It's about gathering information. Can we use the victim for our own campaign of misdirection? Can we make them believe they're doing vital security work when in reality they're simply being used as a means to an end? Find out and report back before anyone is framed or subject to painful interrogation."

I throw him a salute. I'm *so* into this.

I know what you're thinking. I'm going to be spending today and possibly many other days sneakily patrolling Reindeer Crescent in search of suspicious behavior. I'll be forced to insinuate myself into the extracurricular clubs and observe the loose cannons in their natural habitat. I think you're thinking wrong. Someone else might do those things, someone without spy blood running through their veins. Let Bridget Wilder of Section 23 explain how a *real* spy handles a mission of this magnitude. She doesn't go down the *obvious* road. She takes big, bold deductive leaps and she asks herself a series of questions. Questions like:

1. Who has no idea what is going on in school?
2. Who is easy to manipulate?
3. Who would authorities believe to be powerless and resentful enough to work against their own country for an enemy agency?

At lunchtime, I knock on the door of the teachers' lounge. A shy, cautious knock. I hear a "What?" from inside. I open the door and nervously look in. What a dump. Old carpet with holes in it. Old furniture. Old teachers covered in crumbs. Tiny fridge. Tiny microwave. Teachers separated into cliques shooting disparaging looks at one another's groups. This place should be renamed the Traitors' Lounge!

A few heads turn and stare in my direction. They have no idea who I am or why I have a lumpy silver triangle in my outstretched hand. They do not know the silver triangle houses a carrot cake I made several weeks earlier in cooking class that I literally would not feed to a dog.

"Hi, I, um, I had this left over from my b-b-birthday and, um . . . ," I stammer and flush.

"You brought this for us?" My social studies teacher, Miss Helena Hartsock, comes to my rescue. "That's so nice." I catch sight of some of the other teachers, who are embarrassed and uncomfortable having their little refuge breached by one of the inmates. Nate Spar, the physics teacher, doesn't even try to hide his disdain.

"I didn't know it was your birthday. You never said." Miss Hartsock looks genuinely sad for me through her cat-eye glasses.

"Learning is your present to me," I say.

I know. *I know*. Carter Strike would be proud.

I see Nate Spar smirk. But Miss Hartsock swallows hard, and she's not the only one.

"We'll all have a piece and thank you so much."

I back out of the lounge, my head down. I don't have to see the teachers' faces to know that they will guiltily gnaw their way through a brutal mouthful of my awful carrot cake. And that none of them saw me sneakily place a Tic Tac camera in a position where I will able to monitor everything they say and do. But it's for their own good. If a teacher is about to be set up as a traitor, I will see it and put a stop to it.

I leave Teacherville and hurry to my next port of call. Suddenly, I'm intercepted. Joanna is waiting for me and she has questions.

"What were you doing in the teachers' lounge? Where did you disappear to? What aren't you telling me?"

These lips, however, stay sealed. I try to fob her off with a shrug and a mumble. She is not to be fobbed off.

"I tell you everything," she says. Like that's a plus.

"I gotta go," I say, and scuttle away I can feel those tiny eyes boring into my back. I know she's mad I'm hiding something tiny and insignificant from her. I should feel bad. But:

A) I don't.
B) My plan has a second step that needs to be executed perfectly. And for that, I need a boy.

I head toward the main hallway, hoping to bump into Dale Tookey. Instead, I see the flustered substitute, Mr. D-or-B.

I plaster on an expression of deep concern and trot toward him. The look on his face is like I'm contagious or I'm about to mug him for his lunch money.

"Mister . . . um . . . I think there's going to be a fight in the boys' room. I heard word that something's going down."

"A . . . uh . . . fight . . . Are you . . . uh . . . sure?" He stares at me.

"I'm more than sure. You need to get in there and squash the beef!"

As soon as I say that, I find myself thinking, *He looks like he's squashed more than his share of beef.* Which makes it very hard to keep the grin off my face.

"Please, Mister . . . um, violence is tearing our school apart."

The sub looks like wading into the boys' room carnage is the very last thing he would ever want to do. But I make my eyes really wide and I'm working on squeezing out a tear. So the sub does my bidding. He opens the boys' room door. The aroma wafts out and everyone in the hallway immediately drops dead. I'm exaggerating— but not by much.

The sub holds the door open. "Whatever's going on, it needs to stop right now," he says into the echoey space. His speech is greeted with a moment of silence, and then he's attacked with a hail of wadded-up toilet paper and sneakers. He backs away from the door. The expression on his face suggests that he's just seen something he will never be able to unsee. I do not know exactly what goes on inside those stalls but I've heard noises coming from the boys' room: screams of pain, sobs of despair, demented laughter. Sounds terrifying enough to turn any normal, well-adjusted boy into a fake traitor. I give Mr. D-or-B a friendly pat on the arm. "Great job," I tell him. And I mean it. Mr. D-or-B created the perfect diversion for me to roll a Tic Tac camera inside the boys' room.

CHAPTER TEN

The Fake Traitor

Somebody picked the Tic Tac off the floor in the boys' toilet and swallowed it.

Spool has left me ten messages, looking for updates on the progress of the pre-mission, each showing increased agitation. I am not going to reply. I do not want him to know about the awful fate of his expensive surveillance technology. I want to spare his pink-faced feelings and also I cannot bear to think about it without feeling like I will never stop puking. And now I'm thinking about puking, which makes me want to puke even more.

"Bridget. Dinner's on the table," yells my dad,

displaying the worst timing in the world.

"Coming," I yell back but, guess what, I'm not coming, I'm holing up in my room and studying the hours of surveillance the teachers' lounge Tic Tac captured. Luckily nobody ate *that* one.

You know how you'd go on family outings to the zoo and you'd get all excited to be so close to wildlife and then you'd get there and spend ten minutes staring at a monkey sitting on a rock or a tree frog that may or may not be dead and you'd wonder, *How long am I supposed to keep staring at this until something happens?* Now you know what surveilling the teachers' lounge was like. Sure, there was the controversial moment when it looked like Nate Spar had eaten the Spanish teacher's salmon wrap, but it turned out to be obscured by someone's bean curd soup, so *that* international crisis was narrowly averted.

But as mind-numbingly, eye-crossingly tedious as monitoring the teachers' lounge is, I do not stint from my task. I do not fast-forward. I pause the footage every time I take a snack or bathroom break, and I force myself to stay awake until the bitter end. Why? Because this is my pre-mission. This is where my spy worthiness stands or falls, and I do not want to disappoint Carter Strike or—and it pains me to admit his opinion matters to me—Spool. I want them to know they didn't make a mistake with Bridget Wilder. I am the right girl for the job.

What if *Joanna's the fake traitor?* It hits me suddenly as we're walking to school the next day and I'm half listening to her new list of rumors and outright lies. As soon as the thought pops into my head, I can't shake it. She'd be easy to frame. (She's got a motive: Joanna hates everybody.) I feel the need to protect her from the enemy agency that—in my mind—wants to frame her for a crime she didn't commit. But could!

As she's yammering about some supposed offense for which she'll never forgive the Belgian exchange student, I take a step back. I pull out my lip balm and squeeze. . . . *Wait, was it once for laser, two for smoke, three for Taser?*

I squeeze once. A beam shoots out and slices through the straps of Joanna's black backpack. It falls to the ground and the contents spill everywhere. I rush forward, making "Oh my goodness, let me help" noises.

Joanna crouches down a second or two after me and grabs at the bag of almonds, the rolled-up socks, and the semi-chewed Sharpies rolling onto the concrete. I snatch up various erasers, loose buttons, and shoelaces, all the while looking out for . . . *something*, some incriminating item that might have been planted on her, something no bigger than a postage stamp. I don't see anything fitting that description. I let out a sigh of relief. My pre-mission has just begun and I've already saved Joanna from a lengthy and painful interrogation. I gather up the last of her stuff and return it to the damaged backpack. There's an old notebook lying a few feet away. I go to pick it up. Joanna makes a sudden, wild grab at it.

"Give me that," she shouts.

My spy suspicions are aroused.

My sneakers kick up some dust as they shoot me a few yards ahead of her. I look down at the notebook in my hands. I see the words *My Best Friends* in Joanna's faded scrawl. There are ten names written on the page, girls who were in our third-grade class. Girls she hoped might befriend her. Girls she decided to hurt before they hurt her. Girls she now slanders on a regular basis on her Tumblr. My name is second to last on the list. Joanna pulls the notebook from my hands and throws it in her backpack. I want to say something about what I just saw but the glare of doom she's shooting my way renders me speechless.

We walk the rest of the distance to school in painful silence, Joanna dragging her backpack along the ground by the severed straps, me pondering the fact that I'm the only one of Joanna's friends who turned out not to be imaginary. She may be a fake hater but the good news is she's not a fake traitor.

The tension between me and Joanna has not faded now that we've reached Reindeer Crescent. Rather than endure any more discomfort, I mumble something about how I'm dying of thirst and scuttle off in search of refreshment. I speed toward the gym and then groan out loud. I'd forgotten the friendly red vending machine, cheerful dispenser of pretzels, chocolate, gum, and soda, is now the Big Green Machine, home of vegetable snacks, protein bars, and mineral water. A student gives Big Green a loud kick as he passes. He is not the only one. Students chomping chips and guzzling cola go out of their way to register their hatred of Big Green and its displacement of Friendly Red. Loud metallic *clank*s echo around the hallway after each kick. I stand and watch my fellow students leave dents and scratches in the helpless chunk of metal.

"Stop that!" bawls Vice Principal Tom Scattering, rushing to Big Green's aid. The students scatter as he approaches. "The next student who abuses the vending machine is looking at a suspension!" His words stay with me later while I'm supposed to be paying close attention to my science teacher Willy Cyprus's Power-Point presentation on Earth and the solar system. *Vice*

Principal Scattering thought he was doing a good thing when he installed the Big Green Machine, I think. *Instead of thanking him for filling the school with healthy nutritious treats, the students kick his machine and their parents protest it because it makes them look like they don't care about what their kids are shoving down their throats.* And then I find myself further thinking that he totally matches the criteria for someone who'd be super easy to set up. *Everyone already thinks Vice Principal Scattering's a fake traitor!*

Now maybe this is a case of me putting two and two together and making five, but my spy senses—which completely failed me with Joanna—are once again aroused. When lunch break rolls around, I do not head for the fro-yo place. Instead, I go to the gym, where I find the vice principal rubbing a white handkerchief across the scratched surface of the Big Green Machine. I'm standing a few feet away so I can't quite hear what he's saying but he seems to be making sympathetic, cooing noises to the machine, like a pet owner would to an old, slow dog approaching its final days. I want to laugh but I also don't. Veep Scat is a tall, skinny, balding guy who doesn't look like he gets a lot of wins out of life. He tried to do a good thing with the Big Green Machine and the student body repaid his efforts by symbolically kicking him in the face. Friendly Red was empty every day. Students lost their minds if it hadn't been refilled at the start of the next school day. Big Green has *never* been refilled. It's been kicked and scratched and slammed around but I have never seen a single human being press its selection buttons and slide a dollar bill into its slot.

Until now.

Veep Scat is doing just that. He's tapping in a combination of numbers, smoothing out a crumpled dollar bill, and pushing it into Big Green. A granola bar tumbles down into the delivery compartment. My spy senses are fully engaged. I run toward the machine and snatch the granola bar from Veep Scat's hand.

"Hey! What are you doing? That's my bar!" I hear him spluttering with outrage but I don't have time to explain. I need to unwrap this log of pressed brown flakes and prove to myself that my spy senses aren't just a figment of my overstimulated imagination. They're not!!!!

Embedded into the brown flakes is a postage-stamp-size piece of clear plastic with various dots and squiggles on the surface. I start to peel it off when a hand clamps down on my shoulder.

"My office. Now."

I feel fingers digging in. I look up at Veep Scat's bright red face. How do I explain this? *I saved you from being framed as a fake traitor by an enemy agency?* Would he buy that?

I flick the plastic square from the surface of the bar and cram a big chunk of granola into my mouth.

Bleh. I can't believe he replaced Friendly Red's tasty treats with this chunk of gravel.

"I really love healthy food," I say, spitting out bits of granola as I talk. "I can't get enough of it."

I see a tiny little seed of doubt grow in Veep Scat's eyes. Maybe I'm not one of the anti–Big Green masses. Maybe I actually appreciate what he's tried to do for the students of this school. I feel the pressure on my shoulder decrease. He *wants* to believe I'm a convert to the Big Green Machine and I'm happy to let him think that because it means my pre-mission is a success. I saved an innocent man.

"Tastes good, doesn't it?" smiles Veep Scat. I nod enthusiastically even though I *so* want to spit this cardboard granola thing out of my mouth.

"I think the other students will come around to the benefits of the Big Green Machine," he says. "It's just a matter of time."

I nod enthusiastically again. This guy has *no* clue.

And then I hear a rumbling sound. Is it coming from under the school? Is it coming from inside the gym?

No. It's coming from the vending machine. Big Green is vibrating.

Veep Scat cautiously approaches the machine, his white handkerchief clutched in his hand.

The machine vibrates louder as he gets closer. It's like there's someone inside trying to get out. The machine is *shaking* and tipping back and forward.

"Go get Nash Nixon," he tells me. Instead of running to fetch the custodian, I stand rooted to the spot, watching fascinated as the vice principal starts making those cooing noises to a machine that sounds like it's about to explode.

"Good boy," he singsongs. "You're doing fine. I'm here."

He goes to give one of Big Green's many dents and scratches a rub with his handkerchief and a bottle of water *shoots* out of the machine and *smashes* Veep Scat full in the face. He staggers backward until he hits the wall and his legs give way. He *slides* down the wall until he's sitting on the ground, which is when he tips over on his side.

The machine doesn't stop. It blasts a yogurt carton at him. The carton hits the wall just over his head. Yogurt—rhubarb flavor, I think—dribbles down onto the shoulders of his dark jacket.

For a second I don't move. I just stand there staring as the Big Green Machine blasts healthy treats into the face and body of its biggest champion. I could watch this all day. But I don't. The enemy agency has control of the Big Green Machine. An innocent man is in harm's way.

Get in the game, Young Gazelle!

I rush in front of the fallen vice principal. A bottle of mineral water is shot from what I now see is a compartment just above the cash slot.

The bottle flies straight at me. I jump in the air. My sneaker-clad right foot kicks out *hard*. I slam the can back at Big Green, causing a spider web of splinters to appear in its glass screen. Another yogurt pot is propelled at me. Once again, I take flight and repel the attack. Fruity drinks. PowerBars. Kale chips. I kick them all back in Big Green's broken face.

As suddenly as the assault started, it ends. The vending machine stops vibrating. No more food flies out. I lean forward, hands on thighs, breathing hard, not quite ready to trust this cease-fire. But the gym corridor is silent. I tiptoe toward the wreckage of Big Green—and it *is* a wreck; there's glass and bits of food everywhere—and take a peek around the back. With one yank, I pull the plug from the wall.

And then I feel the hand on my shoulder.

"You're suspended," says the vice principal.

I'm what?

I squeeze out of his grip and turn to face him.

"How could you do this?" he says, his eyes filled with sorrow. "I thought you liked granola."

"What?" I yelp. "Didn't you see what happened? The machine went crazy!"

But as I look at his face, I can tell he either blacked out when the water bottle hit him or he refuses to believe what he saw actually happened. He shakes his head. "My office. We're calling your parents."

At that moment, a phone rings. The vice principal's phone. He takes it from his pocket and stares at the screen.

I hear a tinny voice from the phone. Veep Scat's voice. It says, "Good boy. You're doing fine. I'm here."

More tinny sounds follow. I stand next to the vice principal and we both watch footage of me kicking snacks back at the out-of-control machine. For a second, I wonder how that film made its way into Veep Scat's phone, and then I remember Spool playing with the traffic lights on my street.

"Oh," says the vice principal when the clip ends. "I guess someone's been tampering with the machine. I'll have the custodian take a look at it."

He stands for another moment gazing at Big Green's shattered front and then he walks away, swaying slightly from side to side like he's on a boat and the water is a little choppy. I watch him go and I feel a tiny burst of sympathy. But I also feel a big burst of pride in myself because I just saved an innocent man from being framed as a fake traitor, which is to say, my pre-mission can be classed as a success.

I hear the sudden clamor of voices both high and screechy and low and rumbling. A group of girls from the volleyball squad and a group of guys from the football team are returning equipment to the gym. Or at least they were. They stop a few feet away from me. One guy drops his ball. Eyes bore into mine. These aren't the dopes from Doom Patrol. These are the cream of Reindeer Crescent's athletically adept. And there are a lot of them. If they decide to rumble, this could be a challenge for the Young Gazelle. Finally, someone breaks the silence.

"That girl broke Big Green!" yells one of the football team.

The members of both groups break into applause and cheers.

A five-foot-ten girl who looks like she's carved out of granite walks toward me, her face set in a scary scowl.

Even though I take approximately zero interest in school sports, I'm not completely oblivious. This is Pru Quarles, track star and athletic all-rounder. Pru Quarles gets in my face. Or rather, she looks down from a great height at me.

"That machine was a constant reminder to me to stick to my special diet," says Pru Quarles.

She grins and holds out a huge hand to be high-fived. The impact of my little hand meeting her massive shovel nearly knocks me off my feet.

I know I'm supposed to blend into the shadows so I mumble something about having to go to class to work on an important project and quickly rush away, hand throbbing. But I'm not going to lie. Hearing that reaction, even if it was from people who don't know my name, feels fantastic.

CHAPTER ELEVEN

The Pre-Mission Post-Show

I look at myself in the mirror of our pale-green family bathroom. These yogurt stains and little bits of granola flakes I keep finding stuck to my hair and inside my sneakers are my battle scars. My souvenirs of a successful mission. I give my reflection a proud salute and then I step into the shower. When I come out, I hope to find my phone filled with congratulatory emails from Spool and, perhaps, from Carter Strike. I've spent most of the afternoon following my destruction of Big Green anticipating one or both of them telling me how I surpassed their expectations, how no agent, certainly not one of my tender years, has ever shown so much potential straight out of the gate, how they're already talking about nominating me for Section 23 Employee of the Month, if such a thing exists. Instead I got *nothing*. Not even a thumbs-up emoji.

Shower over, remaining Big Green debris removed from my person, I open the bathroom door to find my sister, Natalie, sauntering inside. We both jump and smile at each other. I notice a little streak of white in her hair. I hope she's not dyeing it. Not because it wouldn't suit her: history has proven that *everything* suits her. But it would mean a tidal wave of Reindeer Crescent students with white hair. As I pass her, I sniff the air.

"Is it me? Do I smell?" she says.

"Only of vanilla and the morning dew," I assure her.

But I'm lying. She smells of something else. An aroma that is very familiar to me but not enough that I know why.

Back in my bedroom, I immediately check my phone. *Nothing from Spool! Nothing from Carter Strike. I saved a fake traitor! Where's my applause and standing ovation?*

I hurry over to my laptop. Maybe there's an email from Section 23?

Nope. I occupy myself with other important matters. Should I email Joanna about the thing that happened earlier today? Should I tell her not to be embarrassed about the best friend list? That I don't even feel slighted I placed next to last on a list of people she wished were her friends? That her carrying around the notebook means that deep down she wanted me to see it? Or do I act like the whole incident never occurred? I showed no fear confronting a haywire vending machine but I dread the notion of facing Joanna, so guess which option I'm picking? (The non-Joanna one.)

I go back to checking my phone. Nothing from Spool. I do, however, notice that the feed from my Tic Tac camera in the teachers' lounge is still active. It's after school so there's nothing going on. I need to find another excuse, possibly carrot cake related, to get back in there and remove the camera.

Wait.

Something is happening in the teachers' lounge. Someone has entered the room. Someone who should not be there. Someone clad in a black hoodie, face obscured, with a white D and P on his sleeve. He pulls out a spray can. I feel my blood run cold while at the exact same time, my face burns bright red. The Doom Patrol guy selects the perfect target. The fridge door. Rotten to the core he may be, but this Doom Patrol guy knows his audience. The teachers' entire existence revolves around that fridge. Now, it'll remind them every day that an intruder violated their inner sanctum. Just before the fridge is defaced, another hoodie-clad intruder barges into the lounge. He sees the first guy, shakes his head, grabs him roughly by the shoulder, and tries to drag him away. The first guy resists and they have this moment where they both get up in each other's face like they want to fight, but neither of them actually do anything about it so they obviously don't really want to fight. No sooner has this big angry confrontation started than it's over. Both boys shove each other as they leave the lounge.

So what do I do? My initial inclination is to do nothing. But that's the inclination of Bridget Wilder, Invisible Girl. Not Bridget Wilder, operative of Section 23, daughter of Special Agent Carter Strike. This Bridget Wilder is ready to run headfirst into trouble and say, "Look out, trouble, you're about to be gored by a Young Gazelle!" (Are gazelles actually capable of goring their foes? I don't know but I like the imagery.)

"I'm going to Joanna's to study," I lie as I head out the door. I walk gingerly to the end of the driveway, take a few more steps, and then—

It's a twenty-minute walk to school. I get there in seven. I bound across the streets like a leopard. Dogs break free of their owners' leashes and scamper after me, madly barking at my heels for a few seconds before I leave them panting in the dust. Runners squeezing in a couple of miles before dusk try to keep pace with me. Only one comes anywhere close. Casey Breakbush's mom. I usually see her behind the wheel of her white SUV when she's carpooling Casey's friends to school. I used to think she *was* one of Casey's friends. Now that she's sweating and straining to keep up with me I see the effort needed to create that impression. I can tell she's a little bit impressed, a little bit intimidated, and a little bit annoyed by this speedy stranger in the black-and-gold tracksuit. I could totally make her feel better about herself by telling her she's in knockout shape whereas I have to rely on scientifically enhanced shoes to do all the work. But I'm on a mission. Instead, I say nothing and shoot past her so fast I bet I look like a blur. I'm about half a block away from school when I see a big bright-red skull grinning right at me.

The Doom Patrol guy who tried to tag the teachers' lounge is compensating by spraying big bright-red grinning skulls on the walls and windows of the school. A second DP guy works his artistic magic on the front doors. A third is spraying his crew's name on the ground. Another one has unfurled the school flag. He adds the name DOOM PATROL to the school insignia. And one final genius is defacing the school sign so it reads DEER SCENT MIDDLE SCHOOL, which, okay, is sort of funny. They work quickly and quietly.

I do not.

"Stop right now," I command.

A couple of Doom Patrol guys look my way. They don't recognize me at first. Then the recollection sets in. The Dale Tookey Incident. They swap *Her again?* looks. The head honcho, the one who called me cute, albeit in the form of a threat, takes the lead again.

"You . . . ," he begins.

I don't have time for this. I point a finger in his direction.

"You, I'm going to make cry." I pull out my phone. "And it will be captured on video and sent worldwide. Think of the implications."

Before he can reply, I point at the guy who was adding his spray-paint signature to the ground. "You, I'm going to leave without teeth. Maybe you'll end up with implants. Maybe you'll have to get your jaw wired. Either way, it's going to be uncomfortable."

I turn my attention to the next guy. "You . . ."

These are empty threats, by the way; I don't know if

I'm capable of meting out the punishments I'm promising. However, I have the element of surprise and the memory of the Dale Tookey Incident in my favor.

"I broke Big Green and I can break you," I say, mainly because it sounds cool.

The three Doom Patrol guys wordlessly confer.

"She's not worth it," snarls the main dude. Music to my ears.

"This?" he says. "Not over. Not close to being over." By which he means it's over. He knows it, I know it, the other Doom Patrol guys know it. Only one guy *doesn't* know it. The Doom Patrol representative who took down the school flag and is painstakingly transforming it into something that looks like a centaur that has devil horns and breathes fire. This guy has headphones plugged in and he's so into his art he can't see his crew members slinking away.

"Hey!" I yell.

Nothing.

This guy I actually might make cry. I run up to him and grab his arm. He whirls on me, holding the can out like a weapon. He freezes to the spot, mouth hanging open. So I kick it. Not his mouth. The can. I kick it out of his hand and catch it. Pretty cool. He rushes after his friends, his arms and legs flailing. I have another *What would Carter Strike do?* moment. I decide Carter Strike would establish absolute dominance over the situation. So I throw the spray can I just kicked out of the last Doom Patrol guy's hands. I'm sure Spool has a deadly boring nanotechnology-based explanation as to why my throwing arm is suddenly so powerful and so deadly accurate; all I know is I just threw the heck out of that can.

It sails over my intended target's head and lands exactly where I want. An inch away from his next footstep. So that he stands on it, loses his footing, and collapses face-first on the ground.

I watch him go down. I hear the shocked *"Oof!"* And then nothing. The fallen body doesn't move. Carter Strike would not feel remorse and growing panic but, right at this minute, I do. I wasn't planning on actually injuring anyone. Can Section 23 cover this up? Can they make this go away? I think about calling Spool. But no. This is my mess. I walk, very slowly, very cautiously, over to the school entrance, where the fallen Doom Patrol guy lies facedown and motionless, a pair of broken dark glasses by his side.

I hear him grunt.

"Are you okay?"

"Go away."

I exhale in relief. Still alive. Bridget Wilder has no kills to her name.

"Let me help you," I say generously.

The Doom Patrol guy rolls over, wincing. He sits up and, as he does, his hood falls backward, revealing his face.

"What the hell, Bridget?" says Ryan.

CHAPTER TWELVE

Big Brother

Ryan has a cut on his chin and a smudge of blood under his right nostril. He clambers shakily to his feet. I want to reach out to steady him. I feel really bad about hurting him. But whatever sympathy I may have for him pales in comparison to how mad I am right now.

"This is what you do? That's who you hang out with? Those losers?"

Ryan can't meet my eyes. He shifts from foot to foot.

"I can't believe I ever thought you were cool. I actually envied the way you did what you wanted and never cared about what anyone else thought."

Ryan gives me a hopeful smile. "You thought I was cool?"

"Not anymore. If this is really who you are, there's nothing cool about you. You're so desperate to be accepted by a bunch of jerks that you'll dress like them and act like them and do any dumb thing they do just so you can say you belong."

He looks at me, suddenly angry. "You don't know what you're talking about."

I gesture toward the big red grinning skulls sprayed across the outside of the school. I point to the flag that now has Ryan's spray-painted centaur thing on it.

"You're proud of this? Do you and your buddies walk a little taller because of it? You gonna go back to the Doom Patrol clubhouse and high-five over what an amazing job you did?"

"There is no Doom Patrol clubhouse."

"Maybe there is and they never told you about it. Because they've got another big job lined up for you. Maybe they'll make you loot the supermarket next time to prove you're worthy of wearing the Doom Patrol hoodie. You up for that, Ryan?"

"I don't want to be part of them. I'm *not* part of them," he says, moving closer to me. My lie-identifying glasses are in my tracksuit pocket so they didn't get splattered as I ran. I slip them on but I don't really need them. The pain and embarrassment I see in Ryan's eyes right now convince me he's telling the truth.

"So what are you doing here?" I demand. "Why are you dressed like them? Why did you spray that stuff all over the school?"

Ryan starts to fumble for a reply. Then he stares at me. "What are *you* doing here, Bridget? Why are you dressed like that? How did you even do that thing . . ."

Ryan gives me a long, searching stare. Even though I have no reason to feel uncomfortable, I start to feel a little awkward. Then he does a clumsy mime of my cool can kick.

He grins. "What's the story, Bridget?"

Ryan is finally showing an interest in me. For a second, I even consider telling him the truth. *Hi, I'm a spy!* If anyone would be instantly accepting and not in any way freaked out by my secret, that person would be Ryan. But I also fear that, as a direct consequence of me trusting him with this information, he would blow up the world.

"Never mind about me," I snap. "What you did is going to turn into a thing. There's going to be police, there's going to be questions . . ."

"That's what we want," he says.

"Right, you and your awesome friends."

"They're not my friends," he says, and then he shuts up, looking a little nervous.

"Who are they, then?" I ask. "Who, Ryan? Who? Who? Who?"

"Shut up, you owl."

I concentrate on his face. Flickering green data appears in front of my eyes.

Excessive swallowing. Blink rate increased. Chin tucked inward.

Ryan's lying. Which, okay, is not that different from saying Ryan's breathing. But he doesn't usually lie like this. Ryan lies right to your face and he likes doing it. It's fun for him. This right here? He's not having any fun.

"You don't know what it's like," he finally says. "The kid's . . . my reputation is all I have."

I'm lost.

"I'm the troublemaker," he says. "I'm the rule-breaker. I'm the loudmouth. But when someone causes more trouble, breaks more rules, has a louder mouth . . ."

Ryan lapses into unhappy silence.

The clouds begin to part. "Are you saying there's a new bad boy in your school?"

"Johnny Bluff," he spits.

"And because you're scared this Johnny Bluff is a bigger idiot than you, you joined up with Doom Patrol?"

My Glasses of Truth are blank. I've never wanted to be less correct about anything. Ryan looks down at the ground, unable to meet my outraged stare. Then I have a sudden thought.

"Why do this, though? Why here? Why not vandalize your own school?"

He keeps his gaze fixed on the ground, scraping his feet. I can see how uncomfortable this is making him. I don't want that. I move toward him.

"Look, Ryan . . ."

And then I sniff the air.

"Do I smell?" he asks.

Yes, he does. Of something *very familiar*.

CHAPTER THIRTEEN

Devil Inside

Natalie's alarm comes to life. Katy Perry asks if you ever feel like a plastic bag. Natalie's eyes flutter open. She lets out a little sigh, yawns, and pushes the covers off her bed.

That's when she sees me sitting on her desk chair.

"Bridget?"

"Good morning," I say.

She looks confused. "What are you . . . how long have you been here?"

"Long enough to set your alarm back an hour."

Natalie's eyes fly to her clock. It's six thirty in the

morning. She puts her arms around a pillow and clutches it tight.

"Why would you do that?" Her voice isn't much more than a scared whisper.

"So that we can get to school early and everyone will see us cleaning the graffiti when they show up. That was the plan, wasn't it?"

Natalie gives me a searching stare, concern shining in her eyes. "Bridget, are you sleepwalking again? Is that what's happening right now? Is this like that time we went to Puerto Vallarta and you fell in the hotel pool?" She jumps out of bed. "I'll get Mom. She'll know what to do."

I let her walk as far as the bedroom door before I ask, "Who's Johnny Bluff?"

Natalie's fingers pause in midair. Her bedroom doorknob just out of reach. She doesn't move or speak. After a moment, she walks back to her bed, sits on top of the covers, reaches for her favorite pillow, and buries her face in it.

I say nothing. I barely breathe. She's a young girl, a young, sweet, innocent girl. I didn't mean to break her. I pushed too hard. *Being a spy has turned me into a monster!*

Natalie looks up from her pillow. Her face is different. Hard. Defensive. Her eyes cold and challenging. I'm flustered by this sudden display of attitude, but I want her to be impressed by my bold deductive leap, so I show my hand.

"When I came out of the bathroom yesterday? You smelled of old wood, rust, and paint. Like our garden shed. The shed that no one ever goes into. Except Ryan, when he's stealing something or hiding something. But you smelled of it yesterday and you had white in your hair. It could have been a fashion statement but I think it was paint. I think you were looking for white paint that you could use to clean up graffiti. Graffiti you somehow forced Ryan to spray all over the school."

I pause. Impressed by the way I stitched together this story and also scared because I *really* don't want to be right. Natalie remains silent. Her expression remains icy. I curl a hand around my Glasses of Truth in my pocket. I'm hoping she doesn't force me to use them.

"Why, Natalie?" I blurt. "Why would you use Ryan like this?"

"*Why, Natalie?*" she sneers, doing an inaccurate impression of me. Then she lies back on her bed and throws her pillow up in the air.

After a moment or two of catching the pillow and tossing it back up in the air, she says, "Nobody bought tickets to the dance charity marathon. It was canceled due to lack of interest."

Before I even have time to formulate a response, she sighs. "The dance I organized? That I asked you to be part of? That you ignored because you're always in your Bridget world and you don't care about anything that doesn't directly concern you."

"That's not true," I say, my voice high and squeaky.

"It wasn't just you this time," she says. "Every time I've ever asked anyone to come to the other charities I've been involved with or the plays that I've been in or the concerts, they've always come. But not this time. And I thought and thought about it. And I think I just do too much. I think I'm overexposed. I'm good at too many things."

"Wow" is all I can think of to say.

"I know," says Natalie, choosing to interpret my *Wow* in a different way than I intended it. "It's like I'm my own worst enemy. But I can't let it happen again. So, I thought, what's the problem here? The problem is me. So what if I make people think it's not all about me? What if I put the spotlight on someone else? And then I saw those Doom Patrol morons hanging around outside the school and I thought, they're trying to be like Ryan. And then I remembered. Ryan wasn't always Ryan. Alec McGrory used to be Ryan."

Natalie glances at me, waiting for signs that I know what she's talking about. I do not.

"Alec McGrory," she singsongs. "Big square head. Used to bring snakes to school. He was all anybody could talk about. Until Ryan started pulling bigger, stupider stunts, and then all anyone could talk about was Ryan and what he was going to do next, and McGrory and his snakes were yesterday's news. But Ryan has always been worried that someone new would come along and out-stunt him like he out-stunted McGrory."

"He has?" I have never heard this before.

"God, Bridget, it's like no one else exists. *Yes. Of course he has.* So I invented that someone."

"You did? How?"

Natalie takes out her phone, starts scrolling. "Social media just passed you by, didn't it, Grandma? I set up a bunch of accounts for Johnny Bluff and kids from his old school. Made him seem like the wildest, most terrifying out-of-control stunt-pulling maniac in the world. And then made it seem like he was relocating here." She passes me the phone. It shows Johnny Bluff's Twitter account. There's a picture of a bomb site followed by a tweet reading, *That's what's left of my old school. Get ready, Reindeer Crescent!*

She snatches the phone back, pages through some screens, and returns it to me. I look at Johnny Bluff's

Instagram account. It shows a scrap of paper with *To-Do List* scrawled at the top.

Underneath is the sentence, *Establish dominance over Ryan Wilder and Doom Patrol.*

"So it wasn't too much of a stretch to figure Ryan and Doom Patrol would join forces to take on Johnny Bluff."

I look around Natalie's room, with its stuffed toys, trophies, ballet flats, and knit hats. Who, I wonder, recited the spell to invoke the demon who is currently possessing my sugar-sweet little sister?

In a bored voice, Natalie continues her tale of lies and manipulation. "Once that happened, I put another To-Do entry on Johnny Bluff's Instagram."

"'Make my mark on Reindeer Crescent Middle School'?" I venture.

"Something like that," says Natalie. *"Something smarter than that."*

"Something that would convince Ryan and those yam sacks from Doom Patrol to beat him to it?"

She rolls over on her side to face me. "So now you know everything."

I don't know you, I think. *I don't know you at all. I don't know my sister. I don't know my brother. But then, they don't know me, either. They don't know I'm really the daughter of an internationally notorious spy.*

Natalie rolls onto her stomach, sinks her chin into her hands, and gives me a hard stare. "So, are you going to hold it over my head forever?"

I might. But I wouldn't be a good spy if I told her. And she's already a better spy than me, so I better play my cards close to my chest. I get up and head for the door.

"Hey," she says. "How do you know about any of this?"

"C'mon," I say, "let's go paint the school white."

Which is what we do. Me in my slobbiest paint-spattered pants and most raggedy T-shirt, Natalie in her oldest, shabbiest clothes that somehow look cleaner and smell fresher than they did when she first wore them. My social studies teacher, Miss Hartsock, is already outside Reindeer Crescent Middle School, paintbrush in hand.

"Do-gooder," hisses Natalie, annoyed at having any of her thunder stolen.

"Be nice," I caution her.

I begin slapping white paint over big red grinning skulls. Moments later, Ford Focuses and Honda Odysseys start pulling up. Concerned parents and their small squealing offspring make their way toward the defaced walls. Natalie rounds up the kids, handing them paintbrushes and pointing to Doom Patrol graffiti that needs to be expunged.

"Mackenzie, clean that up!" she barks. "Meadow, those steps aren't going to clean themselves. McCakelyn, grab a brush, girl!" (I think she said McCakelyn. There was a lot of screaming.)

Finally, the faculty shows up. None of them look like they want to be anywhere near the school any earlier than they have to. Nate Spar hangs back and acts like he's supervising the cleanup until Natalie busts him with a shrill, "Come on, Mr. Spar. There's plenty for you to do."

And then one of Natalie's little minions—McCakelyn, maybe?—screams. All heads turn toward the frightened girl. She extends a trembling finger and I see the source of her terror.

Doom Patrol.

All of them. Ryan included. Hoods up, hands shoved deep in pockets, slouching toward the scene of the crime.

Tension crackles around me. It crackles in me, also. I'm out of uniform. I didn't want to get paint on my tracksuit or my spy sneakers. I can't do what I did last night. Luckily, they don't know that.

They keep slouching closer and closer to the school. They walk up the steps. They pick up brushes! They start painting over their graffiti! (Except for the DEER SCENT sign. No one's in any hurry to change that.) Doom Patrol's incredible redemption was probably due to Ryan. My spy senses have a feeling he told them cleaning up the school rather than defacing it shows Johnny Bluff they're not intimidated by him and his scary reputation. It was almost like the Wilder siblings worked together to achieve a goal. I feel close to them despite all the lies and threats. I have a sudden thought. It's more of a mind blurt. What if I told them? What if I shared my secret, my huge unshareable secret, with Natalie and Ryan? I'm seriously considering my mind blurt and all its implications when I get a text.

Black Mini Cooper. I'll flash the headlights twice. I look around. There's the car. The lights flash twice. Everyone's painting. No one sees me slip away. I open the car door. I'm immediately blinded by the dazzling whiteness of Xan's teeth and the incredible . . . well, everything about her is incredible.

"Hello, darling," she says.

The power of . . . that thing where you form words and they string together in a sentence that can be understood . . . whatever you call it, it has deserted me.

"I wanted to be the one to congratulate you in person both for yesterday's amazing success with the machine and the vice principal, and the way you took charge of . . . whatever happened here. I was against you even having to take part in a pre-mission. I hate these labels. But you performed. You exceeded even my expectations and they were already high."

That voice. How do you get a voice like that? It's like a warm bath except it's coming out of her mouth.

"We're very impressed, Bridget." She touches my hand to emphasize her point. It feels like the softest glove in the world. With the sharpest, reddest nails I've ever seen.

"And I know your father is very, very proud of you."

Suddenly I find the power to form words. A lot of them. "Have you talked to him? What's he like? When can I meet him? Can I meet him now?"

Xan laughs her tinkling little laugh. "Soon" is all she says.

The car door opens. "We'll be in touch." She smiles. My cue to go.

Impulsively, she leans across and gives me a quick hug. Her perfume swims over me. I find myself back on the sidewalk. There was something I was thinking about doing before Xan showed up but now I can't remember what it was.

CHAPTER FOURTEEN

In

The next morning, there's a cake with my face on it sitting at the foot of my bed. At least I think it's meant to be my face. The hastily assembled arrangement of raisins and sprinkles dumped on top of what looks like a dented chocolate hatbox barely resembles human features. But the words *Happy (Late) B-Day, Sis* are written right there in a creamy scrawl. Ryan wants to get on my good side.

Over breakfast, he keeps shooting me cryptic little glances and nods. As if to say, *We good? We okay? We're on the same page, right? What you saw, what you know, it stays our little secret, right?* I give him nothing. I keep my face blank and expressionless like the Sphinx. Let him sweat.

Natalie skips, literally skips, into the kitchen. "Good morning, good morning," she chirrups. "Look at my lovely family all together, starting the day. We're so lucky, so blessed." She's overdoing it, even by her standards. But I can tell this show is for me. I can see my dad getting ready to grumble about the nagging pain in his lower back. My mom silences him with a *Don't break the mood* glare.

"We are lucky," Dad agrees meekly.

"And there's my smart, cute, funny big sister." Natalie follows the compliment with an affectionate hug. "Now we're even," she whispers, the honey draining from her voice.

I hold the hug. "Not quite," I whisper back. "Kill Johnny Bluff. Drop him off a cliff. Have him bitten by a howler monkey, I don't care."

Natalie gives me a quick appraising look. Her nod indicates she's decided to take me seriously.

"Hey, bozo," I call over to Ryan. He looks ready to pee his pants. "Walk with me," I say.

We step out of the doorway together. I can almost taste his nerves. They don't taste good.

I take his arm and look directly into his eyes. "People already like you. You're funny when you want to be and you can be cool sometimes. You don't have to try to be anything else."

I let him go and we walk in silence for a moment.

"That's it," I say.

He almost sags with relief. He reaches out a hand to muss up my hair. I go to grab it and he squeezes my nose instead.

"Honk honk," he says.

"That wasn't one of the times when you were funny," I yell after him as he runs back into the house.

I have many thoughts jockeying for position as I walk to school. Obviously, I'm still going to exploit what I know about Ryan, but how and when to do it to my greatest benefit? And what did Natalie mean when she said I'm always in my Bridget world? I wonder about Xan and Carter Strike . . . I wonder how well they know each other. I wonder if they ever . . . I suddenly get lost in the fantasy that these objects of beauty might be my parents. I let out an involuntary *"Yeek!"* when Joanna appears alongside me and launches into conversation, as she does every morning.

"I didn't sell you out," she says.

"What?"

"Last night. When you said you were studying with me. Your mom called Big Log." This is Joanna's charming nickname for the grandmother she lives with. "I said you were with me. No way B.L. was hauling that ancient wreck of a body upstairs to check."

"Thanks," I say, anticipating what's coming next.

"So where were you? What was hot enough to make you betray Jeff and Nancy's trust? What were you doing? Who were you with? Do I know them? I know everyone you know. So."

"I was . . ." My mind, previously racing, is now frozen. Stiff. Completely stalled. Nothing there. I went to sleep last night secure in the knowledge that I was an awesome spy: sharp, intuitive, adaptable, unreadable. And now: there's a voice in my head going *um um um um*.

"Whew, it's hot" is the best I can manage. "It's in the eighties already. Aren't you sweltering in that smock?"

It's a pretty good deflection, but not good enough for Joanna, who trains her tiny eyes on me.

"Oh, I'm sorry. Is that a tough question? I lied for you. You should be able to tell me why. Where were you?"

Um um um um.

I could just run. I've got the superpowered sneakers. I could just leave her choking in my dust.

"Bridget, I asked you a question."

I recognize this is a moment where I can make it up to Joanna for uncovering her secret best friend list. Should I just tell her, *Hi, I'm a spy?* Or should I stammer my way through a fabricated response about visiting a fictional relative? Luckily, I don't have to make the choice right now because a white SUV slows to a crawl alongside us. Casey Breakbush's mom—my old running buddy!—is at the wheel. Behind her sit her slim, pretty daughter and her slim, pretty daughter's slim, pretty friends.

"Look at them, they're peeing their pants," hisses Joanna. "They know they're going in the Report."

The SUV windows roll down. Casey leans out. She's drinking an iced coffee. After a second she removes the straw from her mouth.

"Hey," she trills. "Wanna ride?"

I glance at Joanna. Neither of us were expecting that.

"I knew this would happen," smirks Joanna. "They're trying to buy my friendship. Not for sale!"

"C'mon," says Casey. "It's sticky hot out there. We've got the air condish blasting, and we're taping our podcast, *What Do You Bring to the Table?*"

"Maybe the girls want to walk to school by themselves," says Mrs. Breakbush.

"Volume down, Mom," grimaces Casey.

Casey opens the door and I consider what's on offer

here. A white SUV. Slim, pretty girls. Air condish. My sneakers have a mind of their own. They start to walk toward the car. Why am I blaming my sneakers? I— Bridget Wilder, the Young Gazelle—walk toward the car. I squeeze into the back. Joanna lifts one foot to follow.

"We sort of don't have room. Sorry," says Casey, before closing the door in Joanna's face.

If I was a real friend, I'd march back out and show my solidarity. Instead, I slump down in the seat so I don't have to see Joanna dwindle away in the background as the SUV picks up speed.

I tell myself I'm actually doing Joanna a big favor here because this is a perfect opportunity for me to act as her advocate. I can totally help her standing in this school by telling these slim, pretty girls how awesome she is and getting them all to follow her Tumblr.

(But I know I won't. And she'll be grudge-carryingly mad for a few days, which means I'll be walking to and from school alone. Or not, now that this unexpected new situation has arisen.)

"My little sister loves you," says Casey.

"Mine, too," says Casey's friend Nola Milligan.

"Is her name McCakelyn?" I ask. The question goes unanswered.

"Mine posted that Instagram of you cleaning the

graffiti off the front of the school yesterday," says Casey's other friend, Kelly Beach. "The one that said hashtag *natalieandherbigsisterrock*."

"You're a smash with the little-sister network," says Casey. "And I was like, How do we not know this girl?" She gestures excitedly to Nola and Kelly. "Did I not say that?"

They nod excitedly. "She said it," they assure me.

I would be justified in replying, "You do not know me because I am not in your insular little circle of slim and pretty people with perfect lives. Therefore I am invisible." That's what Joanna would do. But why make them feel bad for trying to be nice? And, more to the point, why throw Natalie's little-sisterly gift back in her face? Because, make no mistake, *she* is responsible for this. Natalie caused Bridget Wilder to trend among the little sisters of the slim and pretty, which is why I'm riding in the white SUV, where hair is shiny, teeth gleam, and everyone has her own iced coffee. It's a foreign land and I am an eager tourist. (But not much of an advocate for the Conquest Report.)

So I smile back at my fellow passengers and don't even flinch when Nola Milligan sticks her phone inches from my face and presses a recording app.

"Bridget Wilder," she says, "what do you bring to the table?"

"She brings those ridiculoso spectacules," says Kelly

Beach, reaching out to remove my glasses from my face.

"Hey!" I squawk, and bat her hand away.

A moment's chill descends on the already chilly interior of Mrs. Breakbush's white SUV. I feel a twinge of terror. What rule did I just break? I was only In for half a second and now I'm going to be Out again.

"Well done, Bridget," says Casey. "Kelly, respect boundaries. We've talked about this."

"I'm *thorry*," says Kelly in a little baby voice. She gives herself a tiny slap on the wrist.

Kelly waits for Casey to register her approval. As she waits, I study Kelly's pretty, porcelain face. My ridiculoso spectacules start scrolling. **Increased blood pressure. Teeth grinding.** She's making an effort not to show it, but inside Kelly's angry. Which makes me think, maybe this insular group of slim, pretty girls isn't quite as perfect as it seemed from the outside. Which is interesting.

"So," says Nola. "What else does Bridget Wilder bring to the table?"

"I heard she broke Big Green," says Casey.

I pretend to lock my lips and throw away the key.

"Love you so much right now!" my three new friends trill in unison.

"What else?" demands Nola. "Something no one else knows."

I'm aware I'm a new toy to be played with and probably discarded when my novelty wears off. But I feel like I'll learn a lot from observing Casey, Kelly, and Nola. So I do the thing I swore I would never do if I ever appeared on a TV talent show. I play the sympathy card.

"I'm adopted," I tell Nola's app.

"Awww," chorus the three girls.

"It's fine," I assure them.

"Pardon me if I'm being intrusive," says Mrs. Breakbush, "but have you made any attempts to contact your birth parents, because . . ."

Casey points her phone at her mother. She makes a kind of *dvvvvv* noise.

"The imaginary partition just went up, " says Casey. "We can't hear you." She pretends to shudder. "I wish *I* was adopted."

Mrs. Breakbush stares straight ahead.

As we walk into school, my trio of new semifriends continue to pepper me with questions. Have I considered Lasik? What's the significance of the black-and-gold color scheme of my tracksuit? Would I be open to letting Casey, Kelly, and Nola take me shopping and completely reboot my appearance?

"No," I respond. And not just because taking away

my glasses, my black-and-gold tracksuit, and my super-fast sneakers would render me powerless and ordinary. If I allow my slim, pretty companions to style me and I become their little clone, what value am I to them? But if they're seen hanging out with someone as radically different as me, it defies expectations. It makes people rethink their narrow definition of Casey, Kelly, and Nola. I can see by their faces, they get it. Well, Casey does, Nola does because Casey does, and Kelly's a little bit confused.

"Go, Bridget," says Casey. "Do you, girl."

She goes to give me a high five. I'm not going to deny it, I love the fact that *everyone can see this*. People who don't know me. People who generally ignore me. People who push past me. People who can't remember my name. People named Dale Tookey. They all see me slap hands with Casey and then Nola and Kelly. But, as aware as I am that the rest of the school is watching me interact with these slim, pretty girls and struggling to make sense of the scenario, I really only care that Dale Tookey has seen me and that he is now thinking about me.

"Do you like that guy?" screeches Kelly. How did she know that? I barely registered his presence. I was being subtle like a spy. I make a mental note not to underestimate Kelly Beach.

Three pairs of eyes swivel in Dale Tookey's direction. I die a little.

"I think he's . . . ," Kelly starts. Casey steamrolls right over her. "He's the road less traveled. Not my kind of cute, but maybe Bridget likes a little dirt in her sandwich. Good for you."

My glasses register Kelly's teeth grinding away and her blood pressure rising. Casey is unwittingly sowing the seeds of discontent. I don't know exactly what to do with that information—other than leak it to the Conquest Report, which I don't see happening—but I will bear it in mind.

"What's wrong with this picture?" cackles Brendan Chew as I walk into A117 with my three new companions. "How did that midget get in with Kelly? Did you think she was a piece of gum stuck to your shoe?" Hilarity ensues. Joanna chuckles loudly, making sure I can hear how delightful she finds Chew's every utterance. Even my new best friends put their hands up to their faces, a sure sign that Chew is killing them. Sitting on his desk, a smug look on his face, he continues. "Or maybe you're doing charity work, is that it? Adopt-a-Midget?"

Chew hits A117's collective funny bone with this one.

He sticks with the winning formula. "How do I sign up for this Adopt-a-Midg—"

He doesn't get to finish the routine because Dale Tookey walks up to Chew's desk and shoves him.

Dale shoves Chew hard enough to send him flying backward off his desk and onto the ground, where he flops around, shocked and embarrassed. There is stunned silence for a moment. From Chew. From the rest of A117. From me.

"Dale Tookey. Principal's office. Now."

No one saw the teacher enter the room. His face is grim. Dale nods, picks up his backpack and walks out of the classroom. I watch him go. I say nothing. I stand there. My face burning. My mind filled with a two-part question: *Did he do that because he can't stand Brendan Chew or did he do that because he likes me?*

"Didn't hurt," says Chew, clambering to his feet. "I'm indestructible. Like a cockroach."

No one laughs.

CHAPTER FIFTEEN

Assignment

If there was ever a day I wanted to be eating lunch by myself at the fro-yo emporium, today would be that day. But the universe is not working that way. Today, the universe is giving me the thing I might have wanted a few months ago. It's giving me an invitation to sit and eat lunch at Casey, Kelly, and Nola's table in the cafeteria. Today, C, K & N think I'm the most interesting person they've ever met.

"You're the most interesting person we've ever met," says Casey. "We want to know *everything*."

"Do you have a dog?" asks Kelly.

Casey and Nola openly laugh at that. "Who cares if she's got a dog?" says Nola.

"Do you, though?" Kelly persists. "I've got a schnauzer called Stamp. He won't go anywhere near my stepdad. It's funny how dogs just know . . ."

"Ignore her," says Casey. "Let's go back to you."

"Yesterday you didn't exist. Today you have two dudes fighting over you. How does that even happen?" asks Nola. She looks genuinely perplexed.

"Walk us through the whole timeline of this scandalous saga," says Casey.

"Leave nothing out," commands Nola.

I would love to do that—the Dale Tookey part anyway—but not with C, K & N. I would prefer to be at my little red corner table at the fro-yo place immersing myself in memories of every look and gesture I ever shared with Dale Tookey, really examining our whole history for clues leading to his unexpected assault on Brendan Chew. But instead I'm stuck at the most desirable spot in Reindeer Crescent Middle School: the C, K & N table. My phone rings. I have never been so happy to see Spool's pink face.

C, K & N register my pleasure.

Their eyebrows raise in unison.

"Who that?" Casey wants to know.

"That your boo?" giggles Nola.

"My poo, more like," I say. Which is kind of a Brendan Chew—like comeback but, at this stage, it just adds to the whole Mystery Of Bridget thing I seem to have going for me.

I jump up from my chair and point to the phone and then the cafeteria exit, the universally accepted signal for *I have to take this important call but I will talk to you later.*

As I leave, I feel C, K & N's eyes boring into my back. *No one leaves our table,* I can almost hear them thinking. *How important can this call be? Who is Bridget Wilder, anyway? Someone called her. Is calling a thing again?*

"Great job," says Spool. "You went from being under the radar to being the whole radar."

"Wait, what?" I whisper. I'm lurking under the aluminum bleachers at the football field. This is not a conversation I want anyone to overhear.

"A spy stays in the shadows. He doesn't become the subject of intense public scrutiny."

"One, I'm not a he. Two, it's not my fault. I can't help it if people are drawn to me and find me fascinating and fight over me." Even as I'm saying this, I realize how ridiculous it sounds.

Spool doesn't grab the chance to mock me. He nibbles

on his lower lip and then says, "Your new status may not be a total disaster for the agency. In fact, it may grant us access into areas we'd previously found problematic."

"Great," I say. "What does that mean?"

"Remember how Agent Strike defined your position within Section 23? He said your mission would be to identify, profile, and surveil individuals with the potential to become future security problems?"

"Cruise." I nod. "*Minority Report*." (Still haven't seen it. No dancing.)

"We have a candidate," says Spool.

His face disappears from my phone. A new face appears. Tanned skin, dark glasses, thinning dark hair.

"Nick Deck," says the voice of Spool over the picture. "One-time software millionaire. Now being left in the dust by newer, younger, smarter rivals."

"Boo hoo," I say. A little heartless, but it felt like something a real agent would say.

"We suspect Nick Deck might be selling government secrets to keep his company from going under," says Spool.

"Okay. I'll be sure to boycott his software," I say.

"Or you could get us the files on his computer," says Spool.

"How would I do that?"

No sooner have I spoken those fateful words than the picture on my phone changes. It now shows Nick Deck with a young woman.

"His stepdaughter," says Spool. "Kelly Beach."

I suddenly remember Joanna's vicious dig from the Conquest Report. *Keep bragging about your stepdaddy's software empire, Kel. Don't stop just because he's seconds away from bankruptcy.*

The stepfather-stepdaughter image vanishes. Spool returns to the screen.

"Too big? Too complicated? Too scary?"

"What, your face?" My best comeback ever.

"The assignment," says Spool. "You're in his step-daughter's social circle."

"Temporarily. Till they get bored with me. And anyway, I've known her for a minute, and she likes me the least of any of them."

But, even as I'm trying to talk my way out of this assignment, I find myself thinking about how I could worm my way into Kelly's good graces and, subsequently, her stepfather's secret files.

"You've got rock-solid intel that he's in cahoots with the enemy?" I ask. Intel. Cahoots. Listen to me.

"I had rock-solid intel that you were part of Kelly Beach's social circle even though you'd only known her for, like, a minute," Spool fires back.

He tries to give me his version of a sympathetic look. It's worrying.

"Look, Spool. I know you keep tabs on me. You know what I've been doing. You know I found out my brother isn't the devil I thought he was. My sister isn't the angel I thought she was. You know I'm up to the challenge."

Spool smiles. "You're your father's daughter."

"That's usually how it works."

"We need to run through every permutation of this assignment. We need an exit strategy. We need to time the mission from inception to completion . . ."

"Yeah, we'll do that, but right now I gotta go . . ."

Spool looks incredulous. "You have something more important to do?"

"I have to come up with an idea of how to bump into Dale Tookey when he gets out of detention without it looking like I was waiting for him. Unless you want to help me run through the permutations of *that*, I'm out."

CHAPTER SIXTEEN

Bridget's
Stupid Plan

The guy who sets things on fire is there. The boy who swears he's being assaulted by an invisible bully who keeps knocking him over is there. The girl who used to eat her hair and has now moved on to other people's hair is there. And Dale Tookey is there. Stranded in detention with this stomach-churning cast of characters. I do not know if I am directly responsible for putting him there. Maybe Brendan Chew singling me out for mocking attention was the straw that broke the camel's back, whatever that means.

But he's in there.

I walk slowly past the detention classroom door, just like I have the past four or five times, acting unconcerned and disinterested, pretending not to peek inside. But I do look, and what I see makes me sad. The way Dale is sitting, the way he stares down at his desk, the way he holds on to the sides. He has that *If I don't acknowledge I'm in here I'm not actually in here* mind-set. I know that mind-set. I've been in that mind-set many, many times. With Joanna. With family members when they're gushing about what a miracle Natalie is. With the same family members when they realize I'm also in the room and they then fall over themselves trying to find a way to make me feel like I'm more than just a consolation prize. That mind-set takes a lot of effort and it does not feel great. So I'm going to bust Dale Tookey out of detention.

I don't really have a plan. What I do have is a stupid idea. Each time I pass the classroom door, I see Nate Spar, winner of the detention room short straw, with a pile of test papers stacked up on his desk. That stack is there to create the illusion that he is a busy and dedicated teacher. But each time I pass, the stack stays the same size and Nate Spar is directing all his attention to the game on his phone. My plan—and, let's not forget, I was the first to label it stupid—is to fire my laser lip balm through the detention classroom keyhole and vaporize the leg of Nate

Spar's desk. It will cause an uproar. Spar will go running for the custodian. Detention will be canceled and I'll just happen to be leaving school at the same time as Dale Tookey. I'm aware my stupid plan has potential pitfalls but if I stop and think about them, I'll talk myself out of it. So I take out my lip balm and give the bottom of the tube a twist. I steady my hand. I close one eye and take aim at the keyhole, making sure to get Spar's desk leg in my sights. I twist the bottom of the tube and . . . *one twist was the Taser, two twists was the laser . . . wait, how many times did I just twist it?*

Smoke belches out. Thick, dirty clouds of smoke. I feel it in my eyes and the back of my throat. I go to rub my eyes and drop the lip balm. I think I feel it underfoot but I'm too busy rubbing at my streaming eyes to grope for it. So much for my stupid plan.

The smoke fills the hallway. Within seconds, alarm bells begin to ring. The detention classroom door opens. Nate Spar comes running out, waving his stack of test papers to clear the smoke. The rest of the detentionees hurry after him. I feel a hand touch my elbow.

"Don't just stand there like a pile of old clothes," says Dale Tookey as he guides me away from the smoke.

"So what were you doing?" he asks when we're out in the school yard, waiting for the fire bells to stop clanging.

"When, exactly?"

"In there." He nods at the school. "When I was in detention and I saw you walking back and forth and peering inside."

"I think you're mistaken," I say. I was subtle like a spy!

"Whatever." He shrugs. "What's the deal with the smoke?"

I say nothing. But I'm starting to think about the potential repercussions of my stupid plan. What if someone finds my lip balm? What if they dust it for prints? What if they take it to the guys in forensics and the finger points straight in my direction? What's the procedure here? Does Section 23 step in to protect its best and brightest or do they abandon us once our cover's blown and we're nothing but liabilities? What would Carter Strike do?

"So now we're even," Dale suddenly says.

"Excuse me?"

"I didn't ask you to do that thing you did for me, but you seemed to think I wanted you to do it. And I did something for you. So we're even."

On the one hand. *Yessss, he did it for me!* On the other hand . . . *even? Really?*

"Even? Really? That's what you think? There's no

difference in your mind between the way I swooped in and saved the day and the way you shoved an idiot off a desk? I mean, I showed incredible courage facing a gang of intimidating thugs using only my amazing acrobatic skill and you . . ."

I mime shoving Brendan Chew off his desk. Even pushing my palms against the air brings a smile to my face.

"So we're not even?" frowns Dale. "I have to do something even more courageous and acrobatic and save you from an even more intimidating group of thugs?"

"We're even," I say. "'Cause, obviously, that's never going to happen."

And with that, I walk away.

I wish Spool had supplied me with some gadget that lets me know if people are staring after me because of the unforgettable impression I make on them. But until such a thing exists, I'm going to tell myself Dale Tookey is doing just that.

CHAPTER SEVENTEEN

Tiny Dancer

"What do you mean, you lost the lip balm?"

"It didn't work, who cares?"

"It's in beta."

"Can't you make another one?"

"You need to retrieve the original. What if it falls into the wrong hands?"

"Relax, I bet it's been dumped in the trash and recycled by now."

"But what if . . . ?"

There's a knock on my door. I make Spool's pink face vanish.

"Come in," I say.

The door opens and my father enters, accompanied by his serious face.

"We need to talk, Bridget," he says.

First thought: *What did I do wrong?* Second thought: *What does he know?*

Dad looks at the lights around my door and windows.

"Have these been on since last Christmas? Or are they early for next Christmas?"

He knows nothing.

"What's up, *señor*?"

Dad sighs and sits down on the end of my bed. "I feel bad, Bridget."

"I feel bad you feel bad," I offer.

"About your birthday. I feel bad about your birthday. Missing it. Forgetting about it."

"It's fine," I say.

"It's not. We threw something together at the last minute. Mom couldn't make it. I slept through the movie. Joanna was excavating for bits of popcorn in her teeth and we had to spring Ryan from the pen. It was a poor excuse for a birthday. I don't want that to be what you have to look back on."

He gives me a long sad look, then adds, "I had lunch with Harmon today."

"The guy with the back?"

Dad nods. I can see he's surprised. That's right, buddy, Christmas lights *and* a flawless memory.

"He sees his kids every other weekend. They do the exact same thing every time. Chuck E. Cheese and then a movie. I don't want us to be like that."

I feel my stomach clench. "Are you and Mom . . . is everything okay?"

"Oh, no. No, no, no. Everything's good. We're fine."

No green scroll in my glasses. I sigh with relief.

"I just don't want us to ever get to a place where we've got nothing in common and have nothing to say to each other. Bridget, I don't want you to ever think I'm taking you for granted."

"I don't think that." *I totally think that. Or I did. B.C.S. (Before Carter Strike.)* Now I *want* to be invisible and unknowable. The unseen observer who lurks in the shadows and knows everyone's darkest secrets.

"I'd like a do-over," Dad says. "I want another shot at giving you a be-all end-all birthday."

He's full of surprises today. Dad reaches into the back pocket of the gray sweatpants that seem to materialize around him as he enters the house. He pulls out a white envelope and passes it to me. I tear open the envelope and pull out two tickets to the next original performance by the American Contemporary Ballet company.

"It's Saturday night at eight," he says. "I hope you're free."

When I was young, like five or six, I went through a little bit of a ballet phase. It could have been that even then I had a yearning to express myself and broaden my horizons. It could also be that I was hungry for the discipline and the etiquette of the art form. It could even be that I got inexplicably insanely, irrationally obsessed with *Barbie in The Nutcracker*—don't laugh!—to the point I'd throw a shrieking tantrum if anyone even dared breathe when it was on. Whatever the reason, I was possessed by the notion that I belonged in a tutu and ballet shoes. That I would be weightless and airborne and graceful. To give Mom and Dad their due, they signed little Bridget up for a series of Saturday morning lessons and, as a special treat, they bought tickets to a performance by the American Contemporary Ballet company. I was beyond excited. Nothing could convince me I wasn't about to blossom into a young ballet phenomenon.

And then I broke my toe. During my very first lesson. In front of everyone. I tried to impress the teacher and the rest of my class by displaying my prowess *en pointe*. Did I slip? Did a jealous rival sabotage me? I may never get to the bottom of it. But my future, my ambition, and my dignity all dribbled down the drain that fateful morning. My tutu and shoes were buried in the depths of my closet. *Barbie in The Nutcracker* got dumped in the trash and, despite entreaties from Mom and Dad, those tickets to the ballet went unused. I hadn't thought about that in years. But Dad obviously had. Just the idea that he remembered how much ballet once meant to me brings it all back, and I suddenly feel a tremendous burst of regret for walking—limping—away from that one class and not trying again. And now, ironically, I actually am weightless and airborne and graceful. I find myself thinking that maybe Spool could come up with some kind of nanomagic that could make me dance as well as I run and kick. Maybe it's not too late for me. Misty Copeland didn't take up ballet till she was thirteen.

"If it's not your thing anymore, we can do something else," Dad says.

"This is actually unbelievably thoughtful," I try to say. Except it comes out something like, "This is actually un-un-un-ooo-hoo-hoo," because of the effort it takes me not to cry.

"So I did the right thing? You want to go?"

I start to say, "I can't wait." But it comes out, "I can't

woo-woo-woo . . . ," so I point to the computer and make a gesture intended to suggest that I need to get back to my homework.

"I'll leave you to it," he says.

I don't go to the computer. I run to my bedroom door and stop Dad before he leaves.

"Thanks," I try to say. And then I just give up attempting to form a coherent sentence and hug him.

CHAPTER EIGHTEEN

Coup

I do actually have to get back to my homework. My homework being figuring out how to wiggle my way into Kelly Beach's life. How do I get her to let down her guard, trust me, confide in me, listen to my wise advice and, most important, allow me to completely manipulate her so that I can successfully carry out my assignment and extract files from her dad's computer so Section 23 can decide whether or not he's a national traitor? I click on Facebook. Two friend requests. One from Casey, the other from Nola. From slim, pretty girls who never knew I existed, who I could never imagine wanting to be friends with someone like me. I ignore both requests. Instead, I search for Kelly Beach and friend request her.

I have a plan. It's a little bit better thought-out than my spring-Dale-Tookey-from-detention strategy. Here's how I foresee this one coming together:

Kelly accepts my request.

I message her thusly: *Boy problems. Help a sista out?*

She responds with a cautious *Oh?*

I display no such caution: *You got right away that I liked him. I knew you were the perceptive one.*

She doesn't want to reply too fast. She waits a beat. Then comes back to me: *Thank U Bridget! I always knew you were nice. I was the one who told the other 2 we should get to know you. Me.*

Again, I don't wait: *That sounds like you. You're a really genuine person.* She takes a little time to flap her hands at her moistening eyes. Then: *Want to Skype?*

We swap Skype addresses. The ringtone chimes over my computer. I click on the green phone and there's Kelly.

"Your room's cute. Are those Christmas lights?"

I give her the 360-degree spin around my living quarters. She shows me her shoes and her dog. Then she leans in close to the screen. Her blue eyes dart around. She takes a breath, steadies her nerves, and then:

"So . . . what do you think of Casey and those guys?"

And that's when the dancing skills that deserted me in my youth will return. I'll say nothing but I'll say it in a way that gives her an opening to let me know how she really feels about Casey Breakbush. She'll say something like, "Don't get me wrong, I *looove* Casey. She's, like, the other half of my heart. But . . . you know how sometimes you can really love someone and care about them and be there for them, but, at the same time . . ."

"They drive you crazy?" I'll say.

And she'll pour it all out. How everything always has to be about Casey, how they have to ride to school with her mom, how they have to hang out where Casey wants and go to Casey's house and watch the movies she likes. Which will be my cue to ask her if she's told Casey how she feels. I'll let Kelly squirm a little and then I'll say something like, "If only there was some way you could let her see how much she'd miss you as a friend if you weren't around." We'll both pretend to think of how something like that could be accomplished and finally, after much deliberation, I'll say, "What if . . . you hung out at your house watching the movies you want to watch, doing whatever you want to do?" Kelly will give this a lot of thought.

"Bridget?" she'll finally say. "Would you want to . . . I mean, we don't know each other super well, but . . . would you want to come to my house some night? We could hang out, watch movies, anything you want . . ." Which will get me into her house. And then I'll accept Casey's friend request and tell her that Kelly's asked me—just me!—to her house, which makes me feel confused and disloyal, and then I'll suggest that I go so I can act as Casey's eyes and ears. And I'll suggest it in a way that makes Casey think it was her idea. So, not only will I gain access to Nick Deck's secret files, but I'll save Casey and Kelly's ailing friendship. I mean, after I've torn it to pieces, then I'll save it. I've got it all worked out to the smallest detail. It's going to be a piece of cake.

CHAPTER NINETEEN

Bus Driver

Kelly never answered my friend request. My brilliant, intricately constructed plan was a piece of cake, after all: a piece of my horrible, inedible carrot cake. Why? Why doesn't she want to be friends with me? What's wrong with me? Does she see through me? Is my agenda not as hidden as I thought? She hasn't just disincluded me from her social universe. Her lack of response is preventing me from successfully carrying out my first legit mission. Which means Spool will be disappointed with me, which means Carter Strike will be doubly disappointed. I haven't even met my real father and I've already let him down.

"Pull it together, Bridget," I tell myself. It's two a.m. I can't sleep.

My paranoia level is through the roof. My brain writhes with worst-case scenarios, all of them stemming from Kelly Beach failing to respond to my friend request. What would Carter Strike do? He wouldn't be moping, whining, and sweating. He wouldn't be getting himself worked up about the ulterior motives of C, K & N. He would be cool, calm, and collected. One plan went down the toilet. He'd simply regroup and start over with a new plan. So what's my new plan? I could utilize the valuable resource that is Natalie. She has the little sister network in her pocket. But going down that road involves giving Natalie power over me. I'd owe her. Worse, I'd have to give up possibly incriminating information as to why I needed her help. I cross Natalie off my list. Now the list has no names. Then I think of another name.

Joanna.

A new scenario forms in my head. A terrible scenario. A scenario in which I message Kelly a link to the Conquest Report. I think it's a safe bet she's unaware of its existence. A Tumblr filled with unflattering opinions about her, her friends, her family, her sense of style, her diet and hygiene. Would that perhaps attract Kelly's attention? Enough to motivate her to get in contact with me? Maybe then I could form a bond with her and start weaseling my way into her father's dark secrets. But, in order to get to Kelly's dad, I need to be able to mess with Kelly's head, and in order to accomplish that proud feat, I have to throw Joanna under the bus. Delete that: I have to drive the bus over Joanna. Then I have to reverse back over her and, just to make sure there are no remaining signs of life, no involuntary twitches or gasps, I have to squish her one last time. Am I up to driving that bus? I wouldn't class what Joanna and I have as one of the all-time great friendships, but she's never deliberately put me in harm's way. If I do this, I can't say the same. But then in a twisted kind of way, I would be giving her what she's always wanted and deluded herself that she had. An audience.

It's two thirty a.m. and I can't sleep. I swaddle myself in my comforter and sit at my desk staring at Kelly's Facebook page. Maybe she didn't see my friend request. Maybe she was sick. I cut and paste the link to the Conquest Report into Kelly's message box. I hit send. Then I make a gun shape with my fingers and point it at my forehead.

What have I done?

★ ★ ★

Oh, Katy Perry blaring through my wall, I *do* feel like a plastic bag, a plastic bag filled with guilt and shame and fear. It's seven fifteen a.m. The computer sits on my desk like a ticking time bomb. I don't look at it. I don't acknowledge its presence. But I know it's there and it knows I know it's there. And it knows pretty soon I won't be able to stop myself from switching it on and checking Facebook for Kelly's response. Which is going to change everything.

I am now officially freaked out. I am walking to school alone because Joanna is still mad at me, and I have heard not a single word from Kelly. What if the shock of reading Joanna's Tumblr was too much for her? Oh my God, what if reading the Conquest Report killed her? And I sent her the link. Her blood is on my hands!

I'm so consumed by my possible culpability in the shocking demise of Kelly Beach, I don't immediately see her sitting in the backseat of Mrs. Breakbush's white SUV. The car comes to a halt a few feet ahead of me. The door opens. I climb cautiously inside.

"You did the right thing, Bridget," says Mrs. Breakbush.

"Mom, zip it!" snarls Casey. She takes my hands in hers. "You're a good friend, Bridget."

"How could someone who doesn't even know us say

stuff like that about us?" shudders Nola. She looks genuinely perplexed.

"Thanks for sending me the link, Bridget," says Kelly. "Pretty crazy. Do you know the girl behind it?"

"She's been taken care of," Mrs. Breakbush says quickly, before Casey can shut her up. Casey contents herself with rolling her eyes in disgust at her mom.

"We sent the Tumblr to the principal," says Casey. "Action's being taken."

Oh my God. Oh my God. I am the bus driver. I rolled right over Joanna and now action's being taken. What kind of action? How much power can Casey Breakbush's mom seriously wield?

"Are you okay?" says Nola. "You look like you're gonna barf."

C, K & N regard me with a degree of sympathy but, at the same time, they inch away from me in case whatever's causing this reaction might in some way infect them.

"Should I pull over?" asks Mrs. Breakbush. A text appears on my Spool-phone. It's from Joanna. *Won't be in school today. Told to stay home. Trouble.*

"Can you pull over?" I ask Mrs. Breakbush. Then I jump out and I actually physically throw up.

Mrs. Breakbush, clearly relishing the chance to act like a concerned mother to *someone*, insists I sit up front with her and attempts to console with me with tales of her many experiences in the world of uncontrollable vomiting. Even without the benefit of a special Spool gadget, I can almost hear Casey, Kelly, and Nola's eyes rolling up into the backs of their skulls. When we reach the school, I have some trepidation that C, K & N will administer a puke-related shunning. But it doesn't happen. In the hallway, Kelly takes my arm. "You're a mess, " she says. "Let's get you cleaned up."

She guides me into the girls' bathroom and points at a sink. Obediently, I turn on the cold water, take off my glasses, and wash my still-burning face. I could wash for a week and I wouldn't wipe away the guilt I'm feeling right now. As I keep washing, Kelly says, "You were smart to send me that link first. Casey couldn't have handled it. She'd have been devastated. At least I was able to break it to her gently and spare her feelings."

I fumble for a paper towel, wipe my face, and blow my nose. And then I say, "I knew you'd be able to handle it. I knew you were the perceptive one."

When I put my glasses on, I see Kelly gazing at me. "Thank you, Bridget. I always knew you were nice. I was the one who told the other two we should get to know you. That was me."

No green scrolling in my glasses. But that doesn't mean she's not lying. It means she believes every word she says. She leans in close to me. Her blue eyes dart around. She takes a breath and then says, "So . . . what do you think of Casey and those guys?" Not to blow my own trumpet, but BA BAAA BAAA BA! (Feel free to substitute your own trumpet noises.) My plan was a good plan. My reading of Kelly Beach was accurate. Resenting Casey fills her every waking moment. She's been waiting for the right time to assert her freedom. She just hasn't had the opportunity or the right accomplice. Until now. Until me. By the time we leave the bathroom and make our way to A117, I'm sure Kelly's already thinking about herself as an ex-member of C, K & N. And she's thinking about me as a smart and trusted friend and confidante. Which causes me to think of the last girl who thought of me that way. I break away from Kelly and drive my bus of shame straight back to the bathroom.

CHAPTER TWENTY

Meet the
New Boss

Ryan's taken to dropping into my bedroom unan-
nounced under the pretense of wanting to hang out
but really to make sure I haven't blabbed any incriminating evidence in the vicinity of Mom and Dad. Until
Natalie opened my eyes I wasn't even aware of the whole
out-stunting Alec McGrory controversy, but now that I
am, he clearly lives in fear that I'm searching his sock-
strewn room for his hidden glue gun and fake diseased
thumb. I can't risk a sudden Ryan appearance, let alone
an interruption from any other member of the Wilder
family. So I'm hiding in the one place no member of my

family will ever show their face. The smelly shed. My dad hasn't been in here in years, and it's highly unlikely either Ryan or Natalie will ever venture anywhere near it since I busted the school graffiti scam wide open. So I call Spool from the smelly shed.

"Do we have an update on the Nick Deck assignment?" These are his first words to me.

"It's going great. Spool, I want to talk to my dad."

"Call Pottery Barn."

"Not that dad. The other one. The secret agent."

"He's deep under cover. The balance of global power depends on him right now."

"He doesn't even have a minute to talk to me? It's about spying."

"I can pass on a message."

"How do spies . . . how does he . . . doesn't he ever feel guilty doing what he does? How does he deal with it when innocent people get hurt while he's carrying out his assignments?"

Spool nods and gives me his version of an understanding look. "When you're a spy, concepts like guilty and innocent don't apply. You've got a job to do and you do it. Anyone or anything preventing you from achieving your objective is a problem that has to be solved. Emotion is not going to help you in those situations . . ."

Spool burbles on. He is of no help to me. He wasn't there in assembly hall earlier today when Vice Principal Scattering called a special school meeting. He wasn't there when Scattering brandished a printout of the Conquest Report (it was the Casey Breakbush fat-ankle-reduction-surgery entry) and launched into an impassioned lecture about Reindeer Crescent and its zero tolerance policy toward any forms of bullying. He wasn't there when I felt myself sinking into my seat as he basically apologized to the student body and their horrified parents for allowing my friend to pollute their innocent young lives.

"It's too easy to call her a bully," I found myself muttering.

"What?" the boy sitting next me said.

"You have to look deeper," I said. "She has no power in her life. No one notices her. It's just Joanna and Big Log."

"Who?"

I turned to the boy next to me. It was Dale Tookey. I felt myself flush a little. I hadn't known he was there. If I had, I would have been prepared to get into an argument or stand my ground if he tried to mock me. But he looked genuinely interested in what I was saying, so I kept talking.

"Her grandmother. See, you don't even know that.

Joanna's just doing what she needs to do to feel like she has a place in the world. She never hurt anyone. I mean, not really."

"She called me uncoordinated, asthmatic, and untrustworthy," Dale pointed out.

"You didn't even know about that before today and you'll get over it," I said. "She won't. This will go on her record. She might not be allowed to come back to school."

Dale looked at me for a moment. A long moment.

"You're a really good friend," he said.

Am I going to cry in front of this guy? I'm not going to cry in front of this guy. (Unless he keeps saying things like that. Which he'd better not.)

I'm making my way to Joanna's house on the pretext that I took copious notes from all the classes that she missed. I carry a plastic bag from the local bakery containing a triple chocolate mousse and a fruit puff-pastry square. My hope is that they might help to ease the pain of this traumatic day. The pain that I caused. I ring the doorbell and wait the expected ninety minutes for Big Log to shuffle her way into the hallway. The door finally opens.

"Hi, Jeanette. How is she?" I say.

Big Log shakes her head. "I never knew what she was

doing up there. I took away her computer so she doesn't make things worse for herself."

My heart sinks. Now Joanna's got nothing. I trudge toward her room, dreading the tragic scene I anticipate awaiting me on the other side of the big black GO AWAY sign on her door.

I knock twice and walk in. Same depressing off-white floral wallpaper. Same worn-thin brown carpet. I think of all the good times we've had in here. It's a short thought. Joanna doesn't even notice I'm there.

That's because she's so busy typing away on her computer.

"Hey," I call out.

She turns and gives me a big, bright grin. I've seen her nasty grin before. But never her big, bright one. It's disconcerting.

"Big Log said she'd put your laptop on lockdown."

"She took my clock radio," smirks Joanna.

"I brought pastries," I say, holding the plastic bag aloft.

She holds out a hand. I pass her the chocolate mousse and a white plastic spoon. She powers into it and turns back to the computer screen. For a moment, the only sounds in the room are Joanna gulping down the mousse and her fingers tapping on the keyboard. I wonder if she's deep in denial.

"So, um, are you okay?"

"I've got a hundred and fifty-four followers," she replies without looking around.

I join her at the computer screen. She is not lying. The Conquest Report has a hundred and fifty-four . . . wait, it just went up to a hundred and fifty-five. A hundred and fifty-five followers!

"It's growing by the minute," says Joanna. "People are sending me dirt about other people so I don't dig up dirt on them. Look . . ."

She shows me an anonymous email claiming the boys' basketball coach has a tail.

The mental image is enough to make me put down the fruit puff-pastry square.

Joanna giggles maliciously.

"Vice Principal Scattering made this big speech in front of the whole school about bullying," I tell her. "Zero tolerance. He was talking about you. So should you really be doing this?"

There's that big, bright grin again. "That was just for show. The principal made a deal with me. Shut down the Tumblr and I'm back in school Monday morning."

I point at the screen. A hundred and fifty-seven followers.

"I'm letting it build before I pull the plug. Then I make my comeback via group text messaging. I'll be everywhere all the time."

She crosses her arms behind her head, leans back in her chair, and gives me a look of pure satisfaction.

"Whoever snitched on me did me the biggest favor of all time."

I smile weakly. "That's great."

"I'd love to thank whoever did it, whoever he or she was. I just hope I get a chance to look them in the eye and tell them I know what they did."

She's *totally* looking me in the eye! Oh my God. OH MY GOD! She knows, she absolutely knows. I don't know how, but she knows. I will not crack under pressure. I'll brazen it out. I'll show no signs of weakness.

Joanna suddenly stands and makes a move toward me. I gasp in fright and stumble backward till I'm up against her bed.

"You going to finish that?" she says and, without waiting for a reply, takes the fruit puff-pastry square out of my hand.

CHAPTER TWENTY-ONE

Best Birthday Ever

My dad—the Pottery Barn one, not the secret-agent one—is as good as his word. He gives me the be-all end-all birthday. At eight a.m. on Saturday, Dad bangs on the door. "Get up, get ready, grab something to eat; we need to get going if we're going to beat the traffic."

"Where are we going? What are we doing? Why do we need to . . ."

Dad pokes his head around the door. He points to his watch and says, "Tick-tock, Bridget."

When I come downstairs, everybody—and by

everybody, I mean my whole family, *even* Ryan—is there. And they all sing "Happy Birthday." Even though my actual birthday is long gone, it still meant a lot. I have time for half a bagel and a glass of orange juice and then Dad herds me, literally herds me like I was cattle, into the Jeep Compass.

"Where are we going, Ryan?" I ask.

"We're taking you to jail," he yawns.

"This is my surprise, not yours. Where are we going, Natalie?"

"I'll never tell," she whispers, and gives me this conspiratorial little smile.

I look out the window. The sign for the next exit says that Raging Waters is three miles away.

And that's when a bomb goes off in my brain.

"Raging Waters? Are we going to Raging Waters? We are, we're going to Raging Waters, aren't we? Yay, Raging Waters!"

Yes, Bridget Wilder, secret agent for Section 23, *loves* the water park. I don't care that there's a forty-five-minute wait for the slides. I don't care that little kids pee in the water. I don't care that the chlorine smell gets in the back of my throat. All the things I should care about and object to and be grossed out by just melt away as soon as I hear the splashes and the screams. Even when I was little and had to wear a life jacket and be accompanied by an adult, I still relished the heart-pounding adrenaline of it.

Today when Ryan and Natalie and I are in line for the Honolulu Half-Pipe, the closer we get to that imposing forty-foot water slide, the less I care about my siblings' fake personas. I am with my big brother and my little sister, and we are all about to shriek in terror and delight as our rafts blast off the end of the huge half-pipe.

Ryan doesn't give himself over to the wonder of Raging Waters quite as completely as I do. Ten minutes into our wait for the wave pool, he starts exhaling in boredom and frustration. Then he puts his phone to his ear and yells, "What? That is unacceptable. We're talking about a young girl's life here, dammit." Ryan rubs at his eyes and then turns to the family behind us. "Sorry you had to hear that," he says. "That was the hospital. We were hoping for better news. But it doesn't look like they've found a heart for this little angel." With that, he starts rubbing Natalie's shoulders. Her eyes go wide with panic and her face reddens.

"Ryan, stop," I say.

He doesn't stop. "It'll all be fine," he says, patting Natalie's head. "God just wants you to splash around in

His own personal water park. Just don't have too much fun before we get there."

The family directly in front of us turns around, their faces creased with concern.

"I'm sorry to interrupt," says the concerned mother. "But I couldn't help overhearing . . ."

Ryan drapes an arm around a mortified Natalie's shoulder. "Don't worry about this one. She's having the time of her life, making every minute count. I guess that's what you have to do when you don't know how long you've got left."

"You shouldn't be waiting in line," says the mother, fighting tears. "Please take our turn."

Natalie gives me a *Can you believe this*? look. Then the long line ahead of us parts like the Red Sea.

"Thank you so much," she says in a weak voice, and then lets herself fall into Ryan's arms so that he and I can prop her upright and carry her to the front of the line. It isn't until we are actually in the water and out of the immediate earshot of the good-hearted citizens of the queue that we scream with laughter.

"Bad karma!" I yell at Ryan. But I am already getting jealous that he hadn't picked me to be the sympathetic dying sister and resolve to take over the role once we get in line for the Hurricane Bay Slide.

★ ★ ★

Three hours later, we're wet, tired, happy and snarled up in the midafternoon traffic. Mom finds a satellite station that plays hits from when she and Dad were young. They're singing along with this song called "Here Comes the Hotstepper." We act like it's embarrassing but a minute into it we're yelling along. After the song ends, I say, "This was a really fun day. Thanks."

"You say that like it's over," says Dad. "We're not even halfway done. Soon as we get home, we're changing out of our wet clothes and getting dressed up for our night at the ballet."

"*Why* can't I come to that," Ryan pretends to whine. "Why am I being punished?"

"Guess what? I've got a spare ticket. I was waiting for the right moment to tell you."

"Why am I being punished?" Ryan moans.

I feel like I'm glowing with happiness. I have the best, funniest, and most considerate family in the world.

My phone vibrates. A text from Kelly. *Party tonight. My place @ 8. No Casey. Freedom.*

And all of a sudden, my glow has gone. The ballet's tonight at eight. I know taking me means a lot to Dad and it means the world to me. I can't not go. But the ballet's over at nine thirty. Maybe I could see the ballet and then sneak out to the party? Assuming it's still going. Assuming another, cooler party didn't siphon away all Kelly's guests. Assuming people didn't get sick from bad shrimp. (A good spy has to take every possible outcome into consideration.) And if it's not still going, when will I get my next opportunity to go to Kelly's house and sneak into her stepfather's office? In the front seats, Mom and Dad are singing along to another song on the radio. Ryan and Natalie join in. I stay silent. I don't know what to do. I'm torn between the dad who wants to make me happy and the dad who, indirectly, needs my help. There's no real choice here. My family has done everything for me. They gave me today.

I cough. It's a quiet one at first. The next few coughs get louder. Loud enough that Mom can hear me over the radio.

"I don't like the sound of that," she says.

"That's what I said, but you keep singing," says Ryan.

Mom ignores him and glances at me in the mirror.

"How do you feel, Bridget?"

"A-OK," I say, and give her a thumbs-up. Then I cough again. Another loud one.

"She's sick," Mom determines. "She caught something at Raging Waters."

"I'm fine," I insist. Another battery of coughs, each

louder and more racking than the last.

"Jeff, I don't think she should go out tonight."

"Little drop of cough syrup, she'll be good," says my dad. He does not want anything getting in the way of us going out tonight. I don't, either. But I've made my choice.

I arrange my features into an expression of abject misery and wrap my arms around myself. Ryan and Natalie both look at me with concern.

"I'm fine," I croak.

"I'm sure you can get tickets for the next performance," says Mom.

"Yeah, probably," says Dad. I can hear the disappointment in his voice and see it in the way his shoulders slump.

"Or maybe you and Natalie could go," I tell Dad.

"Nat?" says Dad, glancing back at her.

I see the rapid-fire calculation in Natalie's eyes. How will this benefit her? What seeds can she plant in Dad's mind? What will she be able to get away with in the future because of tonight?

"I'd love to!" she gasps, and leans forward to give Dad's neck a quick hug. "Thank you so much!" He seems pleased at the reaction. Even when Natalie's faking it, she's still a better daughter than me.

When we get home, I swallow a spoonful of cough medicine and reluctantly agree to an early night. Once I'm alone, I grab my phone and I send three texts.

One to Kelly:

I'll be there.

One to Spool:

The Nick Deck Assignment is on tonight.

One to Ryan:

I never told Mom and Dad what I know about you. Help me tonight and I never will.

CHAPTER TWENTY-TWO

Drive, She Said

"That ladder you use to sneak up here when you're out being weird, go get it. Put it against my window. Then hang out here. Tell Mom you're teaching me to play poker or walking me through *Call of Duty*. Whatever. Something she's got no interest in. She'll buy that we bonded 'cause she saw us having fun today. If she wants to come in, tell her I just dozed off or I'm on level three. Make something up, you're a genius at that."

Ryan puts a hand inside his mouth and picks at a tooth. "And where are you going to be?"

"Out," I say. The less he knows the better.

"Do I get to ask who you're going to be with and what time you'll be back?"

"You get to ask," I say. And then I say nothing else. But I hold out a hand.

"Deal?" I say.

He takes my hand. "Deal."

I go to pull away but Ryan tightens his grip. "One more thing."

"What?"

"When you see my sister, Bridget, tell her I said hi. 'Cause I have no idea who you are."

I give Ryan a big smile. He totally just validated my spyhood.

"Thanks," I say. "I won't be late."

While Ryan is getting the ladder, I select appropriate party wear. Kelly's asserting her independence from Casey and Nola so she's dressing to be noticed, talked, and tweeted about. I'm there to offer support and blend into the background. But it'll reflect badly on Kelly if I show up in my extra-thick glasses and tracksuit. I don't want to make her seem like she traded down her friendships and got stuck with me. I find a party-worthy top and my one pair of jeans with a designer label (Diaper Trash—that's a cool brand, right?). I look at my tracksuit with regret. Leaving the house without it feels like leaving a part of me behind. The sneakers, however, I take off for no one. I hear a thud outside the window. The ladder. Thanks, Ryan. There's a knock on my bedroom door. I almost jump out of my skin.

"How you feeling?" says Mom.

I adopt a drowsy tone of voice. "Uhhh, I'm almost asleep."

"Okay, sleepyhead, I'll let you rest," she says. "I'll check in with you later."

I wait until I'm sure Mom is nowhere near my room. Then, as quietly as I can—Mom has ears like a bat!—I open the window so I can sneak out. To go to a party. And steal information. Three firsts in one night.

I've got one foot out the window when my phone vibrates. It's Spool.

"The assignment officially begins," he says, looking more excited than I've ever seen him.

"Not a great time, Spool. I'm trying to sneak out of the house."

"And how are you planning to get to the location of the assignment?"

"With my feet. My crazy-fast feet."

"A thirteen-year-old girl running thirty blocks at almost superhuman speeds on a Saturday night is going to attract unwanted attention."

"I run all over the place. No one ever notices."

"This assignment is too big to leave anything to chance," he says, deadly serious. "Do you still have your keys?"

It takes me a second to understand what he's talking about. "By keys, do you mean car keys?"

He nods. "The model passed inspection."

I gasp in shock. "I have a car. I have my own car!"

"Section 23 has a car. You have it on loan. I'll text you its location."

"But won't it look weird? A thirteen-year-old girl driving a spy car on a Saturday night?"

"No one will see you. The windshield has been modified to project an image of a more mature driver."

I'm thrilled by the prospect of my car but also a little disappointed that this brilliant innovative technology means that no one will be able to see me.

Okay, now I'm a little less disappointed that no one will be able to see me at the wheel of my brilliantly innovative, technologically advanced spy Smart Car. It's red and white and approximately the size of a thimble.

I clamber inside. I am not a large person. Brendan Chew's Midget Wilder insult, while hideously annoying, is not a wild exaggeration. My skull touches the ceiling of this super high-tech espionage vehicle. I push the front seat back as far as it will go. My knees are still up around my chin. Out of nowhere, the car is filled with the sound of a high-pitched screechy voice.

"Hello, Bridget," the voice says.

"Uh . . . hello?" I say.

"Where do you want to go?" The voice isn't just high-pitched and screechy, it's annoyingly familiar.

"Kelly's house."

"That narrows it down. Can you be a bit more specific?"

Is this car talking down to me? "I assumed you already had the relevant information."

"Oh, did you?" snarks the car in a voice I feel like I've heard a hundred times. Where do I know it from?

"Kelly Beach. Her stepfather is Nick Deck. They live at 1078 . . ."

"I know where they live," snaps the car.

The engine starts. The car makes a left-turn signal and starts to pull away from the curb.

"So that's what you're wearing," says the car.

"What's wrong with it?" I say defensively.

"Well, if you have to ask," says the car, sounding smug. And then I recognize the voice.

"Shut up!" I yell.

"You shut up," the car responds.

"Is that supposed to be me? I don't sound anything like that."

"Mr. Spool sampled a few of your sentences to create my voice."

"I don't like it."

"Now you know how Mr. Spool feels when he has to talk to you."

I shake my head at the irritating voice. "Mr. Spool. Butt-kisser. Butt-kissing car."

The egg-size Smart Car waits at a red light. The car opposite is a bright blue Jeep Compass.

Our car. The Wilder family car. Dad sits behind the wheel. Natalie is beside him. I yelp with fright and try to squeeze down in my seat.

"They can't see you, dummy," says the car.

That's right. They can't. They see the lucky driver of a car scarcely bigger than a shoe.

I watch them for a moment.

They're all dressed up for their night at the ballet. But they're both eating Carl's Jr. burgers. A little junk food before the culture. Except they're nowhere near the theater. My spy senses kick in. The light turns green. Dad drives away.

"Follow that car," I command.

"What?" says the car.

"That Jeep Compass, the blue one. Follow it."

"Why?" says the car. God, that voice is annoying. Do I really sound like that?

"Because I'm telling you to," I say, in what I hope is a lower, less grating tone.

"Okay. But it's not part of the assignment."

"I decide what is and isn't part of the assignment," I say firmly.

"'I decide what is and isn't part of the assignment,'" says the car, mocking me with a squeaky imitation.

I turn on the radio to drown out the annoying voice of the car. I skip a few stations before I come across "Who Wants to Live Forever" by Queen, aka the first song I ever learned to play on the flute. It immediately vanishes to be replaced by some booty club thump music.

"Hey!" I say, annoyed.

"I hate that song," says the car.

I change the station back. The car changes it again. I lapse into sullen silence and watch the Jeep Compass as it makes its way to . . . the multiplex.

Dad and Natalie are not going to the American Contemporary Ballet. They're going to a movie! They totally lied. I'm not sure what to think about this.

The car yawns. "Okay. Seen everything you want to see? Can we go now?"

I'd like to stay and monitor my father and my sister. I'd like to know what movie they're seeing. I'd like to know what story they're coordinating between them. I think about all the ballet questions I'm going to ask them later tonight. But I'm ready for the assignment.

"Let's party," I tell the car.

The car doesn't move.

"Kelly Beach's house. 1078 . . ."

The car judders to life. "I know," it says. "I just like messing with you."

CHAPTER TWENTY-THREE

Bad Company

I pat my hair into place or as close as it's going to get, check my teeth in the rearview for accumulated gunk, breathe on my hand, and smooth out my party-worthy top. I take a deep breath.

"How do I look?" I ask the car.

No response.

"*Now* you say nothing?"

"You did your best. That's all anyone can ask."

"Thanks, I think."

"Good luck," the car says. "Don't freak out and lock

yourself in the bathroom 'cause there's too many people you don't know."

"It's been years since I did that."

"Two years."

I hate the car. I pull my squashed limbs out and slam the door extra hard. I take a quick glance at the street I'm on. It is, of course, spotless, with lawns the rich, deep kind of green you only see on high-definition TVs. There are no lost dog posters on this street. No abandoned yard sale boxes. Then I see Kelly's house. On a street of big houses, *hers* is a big house. A really big, posh house. No new paint job needed. There are two big columns out front and lots of stairs to walk up.

"Don't trip," I tell myself as I begin the ascent to Kelly's front door. I'm halfway there when my phone vibrates.

Casey.

Do I let it go to voice mail or deal with it now? I have to maintain my loyalty and trustworthiness to both parties.

"Hi, Casey."

"Are you there yet? What's she wearing? Who else is there? Has anyone asked why me and Nola aren't there?"

"I'm just walking up the steps as we speak."

"Why does she need so many steps? That's so unnecessary."

"And pretentious," I say, playing along. Can steps be pretentious?

"And pretentious," agrees Casey. "I've always thought that. Good luck. Have fun."

"I will."

"But not too much fun."

"I won't."

"And keep me up to speed. Instagram me, Vine me, tweet me, text me."

"I will."

Casey ends the call. I go to bang the big brass door knocker. No need. The door opens and Kelly, resplendent in a bright yellow dress, stands in the doorway, arms open for a hug. I go to hug her. She turns away and motions me to follow her into the large imposing house.

"I thought it would be bigger" is what I want to say as Kelly gives me a quick whirl around her home, but I fear jokes fall on stony ground where she's concerned, so I make do with an all-purpose "Wow."

"You're wow-ing at my mom's taste and Nick Deck's money," says Kelly. "I hope he's up there making more with that big brain of his." She gestures upstairs. I make a mental note of the general area in which I can expect to find his office. "Or maybe he's away at some conference. Who knows with that guy?"

I trot obediently after Kelly and I see people I sort of recognize from school. Some sit on the stairs. Others sprawl in the living room. Being a good double agent, I sneak out my Spool-phone, capture a few candids of Kelly's party guests, and shoot them off to Casey. Kelly doesn't notice. She's too busy playing tour guide. She leads me into the sumptuous living room and walks toward the French doors.

"*Voilà*," she says as she makes a big deal of opening them on to what looks like a little island paradise, complete with palm trees, bamboo furniture, an overstuffed red velvet couch, and a very inviting pool.

My phone vibrates. A text from Casey. *Did she say voila when she unveiled their backyard? So pretentious.*

Kelly catches me looking at the phone.

"Who's that?

"Nobody. Sorry."

Kelly leads me past the pool to a gate at the bottom of the garden. She unlatches it. A tennis court is on the other side. An entire tennis club is beyond that.

"You play?" Kelly asks.

I don't, but I'm guessing my black-and-gold tracksuit does. I nod. "A little."

"Trying to psych me out," she smiles.

The phone vibrates again. Another text from Casey.

Has she done that whole, Oh look, there's a private tennis club attached to my parents' property so they made us members thing?

"Who *is* that?" says Kelly.

This is tricky. "I . . . my mom. You know what moms are like."

"Be honest. You don't miss Casey and Nola at all, do you?"

"No," I proclaim with award-winning sincerity. "I never even thought about them. Not once."

Kelly circles her fingers around my wrists, looks deep into my eyes. My phone vibrates. I can't break away from Kelly to see what Casey wants.

"I wouldn't have had the courage to do this if it wasn't for you. I'd still be hanging out with people who weren't my real friends. You showed me I could stand on my own."

I feel a bit better about using Kelly. Maybe I actually did her some good.

"Come and meet my other real friends."

She takes me into the sumptuous living room. There are more faces I sort of recognize. Girls who travel in giggling, gossiping packs. A few guys. One of them has opened a board game on the coffee table. He's setting up a bunch of cards and discs. I give him a bright smile. (I'm not the most out-of-place party guest after all.)

"Everybody, say hi to Bridget."

The assembled guests regard me with vague interest. The board game guy doesn't look up. I want to run and hide in the bathroom (I hate that car; how did it know me so well?). Instead I force a smile and let out a squeaky "Hi."

I see an empty chair by the far window. Somewhere I can blend in and be ignored. So I can sneak upstairs and carry out my assignment.

But Kelly has other plans.

"Bridget's the reason we're all here tonight," she announces. "She's made such a difference in my life."

I attempt to look appropriately modest.

"She made me take a real close look at myself and change what wasn't working. Like my friends."

There's a murmur of interest in the room. People who barely registered my presence are now sitting up and paying attention. This makes me uncomfortable.

"I, um, I didn't say that exactly."

Kelly slips her arm through mine. "But you did, Bridget. You said my closest childhood friends, Casey and Nola, were taking advantage of me."

I feel my phone vibrate. I sneak a quick look. It's Casey.

What's happening? Tell me everything.

Kelly smiles happily at me. "You told me they didn't respect me, that my opinions didn't matter to them . . ."

"I never . . ."

My phone vibrates again.

Kelly's guests are all glaring at me. I feel increasingly uneasy.

"You told me to cut them loose." Her smile grows wider. Her eyes seem colder. "So you could have me all to yourself."

"No!" I protest to the watching guests. "I never said that. Why would I?"

My phone won't stop vibrating.

"Because you're a sneaky little backstabber, perhaps?" says Casey, strolling into the room, holding her phone to her ear. Nola walks in with her, grinning at me. They take up position on either side of Kelly. All three of them have expressions of extreme satisfaction on their faces. The other party guests are variously giggling with delight, texting furiously, trying to explain the complicated rules of their board game, or staring, baffled, at the dramatic scenario unfolding in front of them because they, like me, did not see it coming. But then, who would have seen something like this coming? You'd have to be, oh, I don't know, some sort of *spy.*

Nola comes barging up to me, her phone with its recording app in her outstretched hand.

"What do you bring to the table, Bridget Wilder?" she intones, eyes wild. "Treachery! Disloyalty!"

Casey brushes her aside. She approaches me with a smile. "We were sincere, Bridget. We wanted to be friends. But we're a tight little circle. So we had to be sure you were one of us and, as it turned out . . ."

"Treachery!" proclaims Nola.

Kelly addresses her guests. "You know the first thing she told us? 'I'm adopted.' Like, boo hoo, poor me, feel sorry for me. . . ."

"The point is, we can't trust you." Casey looks at the guests. "And neither should any of you. Tell your friends, tell everyone you know, Bridget Wilder is a . . ."

And suddenly the room fills with smoke. Thick black choking smoke. Where did that come from? Electrical fault? Malfunctioning hair dryer? Barbecue mishap? I hear screams, I hear coughing. I hear people banging into furniture and falling over. I feel panic set in. *Take a seat, panic,* I tell myself. *I'm already dealing with despair and humiliation.* I was manipulated by masters— mistresses?—of deception (of course, it might have helped if I'd worn my Glasses of Truth but, honestly, they make my eyes water). I lied to my family after they gave me one of the funnest days of my life. And now I've botched the assignment. As soon as I recall the assignment, panic, despair, and humiliation go on the back burner. A new emotion sets up shop. *Hello, defiance.*

Who cares that I was set up by C, K & N? Who cares that there's smoke in my eyes and the back of my throat and some kid has elbowed me in the ear three times in the past minute? I've got a job to do. An assignment.

I let myself go still. I mentally retrace my steps from the time Kelly brought me into the living room back to her quick tour through the rest of the house. I put my hands over my nose and mouth and carefully make my way out of the living room. I almost stumble into a table. I steady myself and grab on to what I fear might be a human ear attached to a human head. Through the screams and the coughs, I hear Casey yelling, "You're so dumb, you ruin everything." And then I hear Kelly sob, "I knew you thought I was dumb." Hearing their exchange almost makes up for being played so thoroughly. Almost.

The smoke sprinklers are activated by the time I'm out in the hallway. I cough and splutter as water cascades into my eyes. So glad I wore my party-worthy top and brand-name jeans. I hear fire-truck sirens out in the street, getting louder the closer they get. In a matter of moments, this place will be filled with firefighters. I need to move fast. I shoot upstairs and see a corridor ahead of me. Five closed doors. One of them is Nick Deck's office. The sirens get louder.

I hear firefighters running up to the house. I open the door nearest to me. It's Kelly's bedroom. A dog starts barking madly. I squeal in fear and back up a few feet. The dog walks toward me. I shake out my wet hair. The dog does the same. Have we just bonded? Kelly mentioned her dog. What was it called? Stick? Steve?

"Good boy, Stamp," I say to the little schnauzer. He ambles over to me and starts nuzzling my shoes. "Easy there," I say. Who knows what sort of damage slobbery dog mouths can do to nanotechnology?

Downstairs, I hear the fire department enter the house. I hurry to the next door. Stamp follows. Another bedroom. I look at the remaining three doors and randomly make my next choice.

"I'll check upstairs," I hear a fireman shout. I reach for a doorknob. Stamp does not follow.

He won't go anywhere near my stepfather, I remember Kelly saying. I push the door open. Nick Deck's office.

I hear the fireman pounding his way upstairs. I hide behind the office door and hold my breath.

I look around the office. The computer sits on the desk by the window. The fireman enters the room. He checks the smoke alarm. He looks down at the surge protector. He gives the room a thorough inspection while I'm still hiding behind the door, holding my breath. Finally, he leaves and I exhale. I spring to the computer and install my USB thumb drive—*superfast, infinite capacity*. I don't have to wait long. The USB is a little miracle. It speedily and efficiently vacuums up Nick Deck's files. I text Spool one word.

Done.

And then Casey, Kelly, and Nola walk in, all looking bedraggled, shell-shocked and, when they see me, instantly suspicious.

"What are you doing in here?" says Kelly.

"What are *you* doing here?" I counter, brilliantly.

"Uh, checking that nothing in our *friend's* house got damaged," says Nola. "That's what *friends* do."

Three pairs of eyes bore into me.

What would Carter Strike do? Lash out? Weave an even more complex web of lies? Cause chaos with a Styrofoam cup?

I start crying. I've held back so many times over the past few weeks I've probably got a tsunami of tears backed up that need to come out. Wherever I'm getting them from, I'm giving an Oscar-worthy performance. C, K & N freeze in their tracks. They all look uncomfortable. All except Nola, who points her phone at me so she can film me at my most pathetic. Kelly, of all people, pushes her hand away.

"Leave her alone," she says.

Casey and Nola look surprised. Kelly gestures to them to leave the office. She starts to follow, then looks back at me. "Dry your eyes and go home."

The moment the door closes behind her, I carry out the first part of her instructions. I feel my phone vibrate. I'm almost happy to see Spool's pink face on the screen.

"You got it?"

"I got it."

"Make your way to the tennis courts at the back of the house," he says. "Another agent will take delivery of the USB."

"That's it?"

Spool looks baffled.

"No *Great work, Bridget*?"

He gives me a pained look. "The tennis courts?"

"Okay, I'm going. But it *was* great work. I cried. I turned the tears on and off. I didn't even know I could do that."

"The tennis courts? Tonight would be good."

C, K & N and a few remaining guests are congregated in the kitchen, yammering about the smoke and the sudden appearance of the firemen. I slip, unnoticed, into the dining room. I head toward the French doors and out into the exotic palm-laden back garden. I walk quickly and quietly down the patio past the pool until I'm at the gate leading to the tennis club. With a little effort, I free the bolt and head onto the empty courts.

And, just like that, it feels like I'm a million miles away from that house and those slim, pretty, popular, devious girls and the role that I was—brilliantly!—playing. Now I'm a lone agent with a USB brimming over with red-hot information, waiting to interact with a fellow professional in the murky world of international espionage. I wish the other spy would hurry up. It's starting to get a little spooky lurking out here at night in a deserted tennis court.

After what seems like forever, but was probably ninety seconds, I hear footsteps. Then I see a shadowy figure. He's backlit by the full moon. I feel my heart start to thump in my chest. The figure gets closer. I clutch the USB in my fist. The agent is close enough that I can make out his features.

"Hello, Bridget," says Carter Strike.

CHAPTER TWENTY-FOUR

Strike

I'd know him anywhere. He's taller than I expected. Six feet at least and wearing a black leather jacket. He came to meet me. He came to surprise me. What do I call him? Agent Strike? Carter? Dad? Do I shake his hand? Should we hug? I try not to stare but, at the same time, I'm openly studying his face. Are there any similar features? Anything that links me to him? It's amazing to me that he's just shown up out of the blue like this. It tells me he's been as anxious to meet me as I have been to meet him. But if I'd known I was going to see him today, I might have rehearsed what I was going to say and how I was going to act. Instead, I stand rooted to the spot with my mouth hanging open. I think I say "Buh."

Luckily, Carter Strike knows what to do. Carter Strike always knows what to do. He strides over to me, takes my hand, removes the USB drive from my palm, and puts it in his jacket pocket but keeps holding my hand.

"You did great, Bridget," he says with a smile.

I feel myself go red. But it's the good kind of red. The *I can't believe how happy I am right now* kind of red.

"I tried to get Spool to tell me that," I say.

He shakes his head. "Spool's aware you completed the assignment."

"I only ever see his pink face. Is there any more of him?"

Carter Strike—aka my father—gives me a quizzical look. I feel a bit embarrassed. Here he is attempting to communicate with me spy to spy, one professional to another, and I'm trying to get him to gossip and crack jokes. I make an effort to control what comes out of my mouth. It does not go well.

"How did you feel when you found out about me?" I ask. "Was it like there'd been something missing in your life up to that moment and you didn't know what it was?"

"I was ready to do the right thing."

"What do you think of the name Bridget? Would you

have called me that? It's not very secret agent-y. Maybe you'd have called me something like Jett? Or Power? Power Strike."

"I like Bridget. It suits you."

"Where do you live? What's your house like? Is there a room for me? I mean, if I wanted to visit and stay over for a night or two. Not move in. You'd have to talk to my mom and dad, but they're cool. You probably know that. You've checked them out. Or Spool's given you the intel . . ."

I'm aware I'm babbling. I put my free hand over my mouth to let him know the leak is plugged. He takes his hand from mine.

"I wish we had more time, Bridget, but . . ." He brandishes the USB. "You did great work. Now I have to go do my part. We'll see each other soon, I promise. Maybe the next assignment, we'll work together."

"I'd love that."

He puts his hand on the back of my neck. I let myself lean into his chest.

"I have to go," he says.

"Wait," I say.

He stops and turns back. His face is already obscured by shadows.

"What do I call you?"

"Whatever you want," he says. And fades away into the night.

"Strike," I repeat to myself about a dozen times. I know I can't stand in an empty tennis court all night. I return to Kelly's yard and tiptoe around the side of her house until I'm back on the street. I head toward my car. I hear footsteps behind me, getting closer. I feel myself tense up. What are my options here? The car, obviously. But what if the car decides to mess with me and refuses to unlock? I could run. But my superspeed might draw undue attention. I could double back to Kelly's house, where I probably wouldn't be greeted with open arms. Or I could engage, show this pursuer they're stalking the wrong girl. I spin around. And see Dale Tookey a few feet behind me.

We stare at each other for a second. This is weird. We're not in school. We're nowhere near the fro-yo store or the doughnut place. What possible reason could he have to be here? Dale Tookey holds out a hand, and there in his palm is my lip balm. He gives me a kind of half smile.

"Yours, I believe."

CHAPTER TWENTY-FIVE

Crash into Me

"What do you call that flavor?" Dale asks as I take back the lip balm.

"Pear," I say.

"Just pear?"

"Smoky pear."

He nods. I'm not sure what game we're playing here but I don't like that I'm not the only one with the secrets. I take the direct approach.

"What's the story, Dale Tookey? Why are you following me?"

"Who says I was following you?"

I hit him with a full-on scornful gaze. "Come on. Why else would you be anywhere near Kelly Beach's party?"

He's uncomfortable. The pressure of my interrogation has him off balance and nervous.

"Maybe I like crashing parties. Maybe that's my thing."

I'm not sure I buy it but I've learned from my Glasses of Truth how to spot deception, lies, and cover-ups. I search his face for signs of fakery. Nope. He seems to be clean as a whistle.

Dale fixes me with a curious look. "I have a question. Where'd you get the lip balm?"

"What makes you think it's mine?" We both know it's mine. I just don't want to give him the satisfaction of being right.

He gets close to me. "Your lips are cracked and dry."

My fingers automatically go to my mouth. He gives me a mocking grin. Jerk.

"One, you were lurking outside detention . . ."

"I was *not* lurking . . ."

"Two, suddenly there was smoke everywhere. Three, I saw you fumbling around looking for something."

Dale Tookey seems very pleased with himself as he counts on his fingers.

"Well, I don't know what you or your fingers are talking about," I say. "It's not mine."

"My mistake." He goes to take back the lip balm. I close my hand around it, and also his hand. I didn't mean to do that. But I don't want to immediately snatch it away and, clearly, neither does he, because he's not moving his hand. So while I would not define what we're currently doing as holding hands, there's no denying that Dale Tookey's warm hand is in mine.

Finally, I open my palm. He takes his hand away. Slowly. That was weird.

"I will, however, send this tube of defective lip balm back to the manufacturer," I tell him. "They might send me a lifetime supply. Or, at the very least, a gift card."

"Keep me posted on how that goes," he says.

"I'm sure I'll have forgotten talking to you," I say. I'm not a rude person but something about this guy is just bringing it out of me.

"I'll remind you. I was the guy who saved you when Casey Breakbush and her friends were about to annihilate you."

I laugh out loud. "That's hilarious. It's so funny to me that you think that. That you think I needed your help."

"What would you have done if I hadn't been there?"

What's with this Dale Tookey? He has barely said a

word, hardly even a syllable, for years. Now I can't get him to shut up.

"We'll never know, will we, because some *party crasher* blundered in like a bull in a china shop and filled the house with smoke from a defective tube of lip balm."

"You don't need those girls' approval," he says. "You're cool like you are."

I'm not sure how to react. Was that a compliment? Or was it a trap hidden inside a compliment? Once again, I search his face with its well-attended eyebrows and slightly chewed lower lip. No sign of lies hiding just below the surface.

"What are you doing now?" he says.

"Why, do you have some more parties to crash?"

He looks pleased. "You want to? Might be fun."

I have this feeling that I *do* want to, that I might like it if tonight didn't need to end. But then I remember who I am and where I am and where I should be by this time

"I've had enough fun for one night," I say. "My dad's picking me up. He should be here any minute to get me . . ."

No sooner are those lies out of my mouth than the Smart Car honks its horn.

Dale Tookey, I can't help but notice, looks disappointed. And not the usual kind of disappointment I tend to bring out in people. He looks like he genuinely didn't want me to go.

"There he is," I say. "I gotta run. See you in school."

I walk away from him and head toward the tiny car, which, amazingly, has an image of my dad at the wheel.

"Hi, car!" I yelp as I clamber inside.

"I can wait if you want to give your boyfriend a good-night kiss," the car snarks. I'm in too peppy a mood to let the car get to me. I carried out my assignment. I met my real dad, and he told me I did great. And then there was that thing with Dale Tookey, which was a little bit bizarre but not in a completely awful way. All in all, a good night for Bridget Wilder.

"Take me home," I tell the car.

The car deposits me in the street behind my house. I get out and everything is dark and quiet. One of the streetlights isn't working properly. It's bright one second, dark the next. I see shadows behind the closed curtains of the houses around me. I'm the only one out here. Just me and the lost dogs. It's late and I'm standing out in the street by myself. I feel the sudden urgent need to be in my room again. I sneak into the backyard and head for the ladder. It's not there. The light is on in my bedroom. Mom and Dad stand in the window watching me. They do not look happy.

CHAPTER TWENTY-SIX

Home

Dad stands halfway up the stairs, his arms folded. I can see how angry he is. Mom is a few steps above him. She looks more disappointed than mad. Ryan is at the top of the stairs. He has an apologetic look on his face. He puts his hands together and rests them on his cheek. "I fell asleep," he mouths. "Sorry."

"Well, Bridget?" is all Dad says.

How do I fix this? How do I make it right? What lie should I tell that will stop them looking at me like this?

"I felt better," I start to say. "There was this party. I sort of promised . . ."

Dad stares at me like he's never even seen me before. Ryan gives me a thumbs-down.

"Do you have so little respect for us that you would treat us like this?" says Mom. "Do you know how much Dad wanted to take you to the ballet? How excited he was to make up for missing your birthday?"

"So why didn't he go then?" I shoot back. "Why did he and Natalie go to the movies instead? I'm not the only liar. . . ."

I see Ryan's head fall into his hands. Bad response? Natalie joins the circle of accusers, leaning on the top of the stairs, staring sadly down at me.

"The movies was my idea. I wanted you and Dad to have your night at the ballet."

Well played, perfect little sister. I've got some ammunition of my own to unload on her but even in this tense moment I fear I'm no match for her.

Dad walks downstairs, face grim.

"Really, Bridget? You don't see any difference between me not wanting to go to something I thought we wanted to do together and you lying and sneaking out of the house . . . ?"

"And worrying us to death," breaks in Mom. "Anything could have happened."

Except it didn't, because I had a sarcastic self-driving

car and a pair of enhanced sneakers and an infatuated party crasher *and* Agent Carter Strike all looking out for me. But I can't tell my family that. I could try tears. But I don't want to. I know I messed up here and I don't want to treat Mom and Dad like I treated C, K & N. I hang my head and say nothing.

"I hope the party was worth it," says Mom.

"It wasn't," I mutter.

"Those girls don't even like you," says Natalie helpfully. I give her a threatening look. She shuts up.

"Go to your room," sighs Dad. "I don't want to talk about this anymore tonight."

"I know. I'm sorry."

"You're grounded for a week."

"That's fair."

"No computer. No phone."

He holds out his hand, waiting for me to hand over my Spool-phone. A wave of panic hits me.

What if Spool has another assignment for me? What if Carter Strike wants to get in touch? Didn't he say we were going to work together next time? I can't be without my phone. I ought to just go to my room and figure out a contingency plan. But I don't.

"No," I say.

"Excuse me?" says Dad.

"Ryan does worse, far worse, far more times than me. You never take his computer or phone away."

"I'm beyond help," says Ryan.

"This isn't a negotiation, Bridget," says Dad. "Give me your phone now."

"Just do it," sighs Mom.

Dad sees my phone sticking out of my pocket. He goes to take it. I grab it back. "Don't touch that," I say, clutching the phone.

I see the disbelief in Dad's face. He stares at me and then peers at the stupid Spool-phone.

"That's not the phone we bought you. Where did you get that?"

Upstairs, I see Ryan and Natalie trade looks of astonishment. They can get away with *anything* after this.

My only solution is to attack. "Of course you wouldn't recognize my phone. You don't notice anything about me. You didn't even remember my birthday."

"That's not fair," Mom says.

"You never notice anything. You don't know if I'm having a bad time at school. You don't know how tough it is being friends with Joanna. You stopped noticing anything after I quit ballet and the flute because I wasn't any good at them, but there might be something I'm good at."

"We're all tired," says Dad. "Go upstairs. We'll talk about this in the morning."

"Where would I like to go on vacation? What food do I like? Am I scared of dragonflies or horseflies?"

"Let it go," calls Ryan.

He's right. I'm not doing myself any good, but now that I've started I find that I can't stop.

"Why did you even want me?"

I see Mom's hand fly to her open mouth. Dad says nothing.

"I know how hard it is to adopt a child. You put all that effort into it and then you treat me like I'm invisible."

"You want to be grounded for another week?" says Dad. "Keep talking."

"My real dad would never treat me like this," I fire back.

"Shut up, Bridget," yells Natalie.

Mom walks upstairs without a word.

"Do what you want," says Dad, and heads into the living room.

I want to run after them. I want to say I'm sorry. I want to walk out the front door and find Carter Strike. But I don't do anything. I stay standing in the middle of the hallway, wondering how I let *that* happen.

CHAPTER TWENTY-SEVEN

The Dentist

I have become a person who plays many roles. I am a secret agent (pretty good). I am a student (average). I am a daughter (disappointing). And today, I am a dentist.

It appears that I have unwittingly turned my home into a dentist's waiting room. Everyone's on edge. No one meets anyone else's eyes. Everyone fears the worst. And it's my presence, my dentist-like presence, that is the cause. It's been this way since I got up this morning. Now I am sitting through the longest, quietest breakfast ever. Natalie is last to come into the kitchen. She has her happy morning face on. Then she reads the room. No one needs her brand of positivity right now. She walks up to me and gives me a big hug.

"You suck," she whispers, voice cold as ice.

Much of the time I spent not sleeping last night I devoted to thinking about what I would say this morning. What kind of apology or explanation would be sufficient to release me from Disappointment Jail where I currently reside? But from the way Mom and Dad are doing their very best to avoid looking at or talking to me, it doesn't seem as if I'm going to be able to deliver any kind of apology or explanation. Maybe more time needs to elapse before they're ready to let me redeem myself. I know they'll come around. In the meantime, the best thing I can do for them, and for myself, is to go underground and stay out of sight.

I head for my room and, for the first time since last night, start to worry about what people who aren't actually related to me are saying.

I check my phone.

A new Conquest Report group text.

Bridget Wilder: The shoplifting phase. The bed-wetting years. The lizard she killed.

I gasp in shock. I can't believe she'd bring that up. (Yes, okay, it happened. But it was a chameleon. They get stressed out if you handle them a lot. Or forget to feed them because you can't find them because they're so good at blending into their environment. So it wasn't technically just my fault.)

I'm not freaking out, though. Here's how I see it: my name became mud on Saturday night. There's a whole Sunday to go. By Monday morning, Reindeer Crescent will be whirring with a million fresh shocks and scandals. I'm nothing by comparison.

I drag myself out of bed Monday morning feeling optimistic. I'm yesterday's mess. Today's a fresh start. I don't see my black-and-gold tracksuit. I grab the pile of clothes on the floor. It doesn't seem to be there but I sort through the pile a few times in case it magically appears. I check my dresser. I check the closet. Not there.

"Mom?"

I hear her voice outside my door. "What?"

"I can't find my tracksuit. My black-and-gold tracksuit."

"I know. The one you wear every day. The one that's never been washed."

I groan. Spool. Millions of dollars' worth of nanotechnology. In the washing machine with Dad's socks and Ryan's T-shirts with the mysterious stains that are impossible to remove.

I throw the door open. "You washed it? Why did you wash it? I didn't ask you to wash it."

Mom is unmoved by my obvious distress. "*It* asked me to wash it. It wanted to feel fresh. It was surprised you didn't want to feel fresh."

"Stop trying to be funny," I snap at her. "It's not you."

Mom's face grows hard. "Don't talk to me like that, Bridget."

Great. This is the first time we've talked since Saturday night and time has not healed any of the wounds I caused. And keep causing.

Dad ventures out of the bathroom. He sees the expression on Mom's face.

"Remember what you said when we signed the adoption papers?" he asks her.

Mom flinches slightly, like she's angry at Dad for putting her on the spot.

"You said, Bridget's coming home." He looks at me. "You were part of this family before you even got here. We waited so long for you . . ."

"How you can think we don't want you . . ." Mom can't finish her sentence. Her eyes start to well up. I see Dad caught between trying to console her and trying to talk to me. This is too much. I want to rush into their arms and tell them I'm sorry. I want to tell them *everything*. But it's too big a risk. What if they won't let me be a spy anymore? What if they want me to stay away from Carter Strike? I don't trust myself right now. Even though I know I'm coming across as horrible, selfish, and ungrateful, I hurry back to my room and then head straight for school.

I spend the long, solo journey to school replaying this morning's events in my head. I know I'm not this awful. Then I hear Joanna's voice behind me. "That's right," she cackles. "That was just the beginning. I've got a million more Bridget Wilder stories. She's like a malignant growth on the face of Reindeer Crescent."

I stop and wait for Joanna to catch up. If she wants a confrontation, I'm ready for it. Joanna walks straight past me, still barking malicious rumors about me into her phone. There's probably no one on the other end. It's just her way of letting me know she's still mad at me.

I wait and watch her waddle into the distance.

Splat!

A plastic cup half full of iced coffee hits the sidewalk inches from my feet and soaks my sneakers. I look around and see a white SUV drive past.

C, K & N. Whatever. They're petty and obsessive. The rest of the school will have forgotten by now. To them, I'm not even old news, I'm no news.

It turns out that I am *not* old news. It turns out my fellow students have long attention spans and even longer memories. The catcalling starts before I even march up the steps to Reindeer Crescent.

"Bed-wetter!"

"Shoplifter!"

"Lizard killer!"

Apparently, people's lives are so boring and empty that they've been waiting all weekend to hurl insults at me. Little do they know, I'm a trained spy. I know how to tune out useless background noise and focus on what matters. Besides, I've been abused by Brendan Chew, a master at the art of getting under my skin. These random nitwits lining the hallway are, by comparison, a pack of clueless chattering monkeys. They won't get to me. I'm too tough for that.

It turns out that I am *not* too tough. They did get to me. The snickering and whispering and texting and Insta-gramming and Conquest Reporting followed me into A117 and then through the rest of my morning. By lunch, the rumors had spread so widely and inaccurately that I was being accused of shoplifting lizards and killing them with my own pee. The thought of a whole cafeteria filled with anti-Bridget sentiment was too much to stomach. So I fled to the library. Which is where I am now. Catching up on my reading. Not hiding.

I'm pretty sure the librarians are talking about me. But maybe that's just my paranoia overwhelming my common sense. I've been trying to get lost in this book I heard was good. It's about a plucky young spy, like myself, and her friendship with a female pilot in World War Two. Every time I turn a page, I realize I have no memory of what I just read and have to go back to the start.

"Miss, uh . . . Miss . . . uh . . ."

Someone's looming over me. I look up. It's that substitute teacher, the chubby, nervous one. I haven't seen him in weeks and I still can't remember his name. Did it start with a B or a D? Whatever. He's giving me this weird look. My hand immediately goes to my mouth. I always think there's stuff stuck between my teeth.

"Is everything all right?"

I stare at him. Is he really talking to me?

"Just, you know, things can be . . . life, school life, can be stressful. If you need someone to talk to, not to judge, just listen, then, you know . . ."

He trails off. My God, this is awkward.

"I'm fine," I assure him. "Just reading."

I hold up the book to let him know what I'm doing

and that it is a solitary activity.

"Good. Fine. I'll let you get back to it. Just wanted to check in."

He gives me this painfully long searching look before finally backing away, and then he walks into one of the librarians, who is just about to put a bunch of books back on the shelves. The books, obviously, fall all over the floor. Mr. B-or-D tries to help the librarian scoop them up. She's even more freaked out by his close proximity than I was.

It's funny but it's not funny. That clown was the only person in my entire life who has been even remotely nice to me today. I cannot take another twenty-four hours of this.

CHAPTER TWENTY-EIGHT

Pru Lies

The Spool-phone vibrates at five twenty in the a.m. If this had happened a few days ago, I would have either ignored it or berated Spool for being unaware of the basic rules of decent human behavior. But, as I did not sleep for more than thirty consecutive seconds last night, I'm grateful for something to distract me from staring at the ceiling and wondering who I'm going to upset or alienate over the course of the coming day.

"Hey," I grunt at Spool.

His face does not fill the screen. Instead I see footage taken from school. From the gym corridor in my school.

I see myself high-fiving the massive hand of athletic phenomenon Pru Quarles.

The image freezes, then fades, to be replaced by the
nonathletic features of Spool.

"She's on the radar," he says.

"What?"

"That girl."

"Pru Quarles?"

"Let me tell you something about being a spy: no one
trusts anybody ever. Rumors are circulating among our
enemies that *you* are the misdirection and *she* is the secret
spy working undercover for Section 23 in Reindeer Crescent."

I'm stung by this. "Wait, why would they think I'm
the misdirection?"

"Look at her," says Spool. "And look at you."

"She's the genetic freak," I say. "I'm the normal one."

"The point is, she's been noticed by people who do
not have her best interests at heart. We have intel an
approach is going to be made."

I sit up in bed, completely alert and completely nervous. "What sort of approach?"

"They're going to try to turn her, make her one of
theirs. If that fails, they're going to pump her for information on Section 23."

"But she doesn't know anything about Section 23. She doesn't know anything about *anything* except running fast and hitting things." That's actually untrue. Pru Quarles is also an excellent student. Don't you love people who are good at everything? I know I do.

"You need to keep her safe," says Spool. "Be her best friend, her shadow, her study buddy. Whatever you have to do."

"Got it."

I jump out of bed. My hand still aches from my one and only contact with Pru Quarles, but I have a mission to keep her from the evil clutches of the enemy and that is what I'm going to do. Truthfully, I'm also glad for the excuse to not have to endure another awkward breakfast with my family. The part I'm looking forward to less is doing laps around the track with Pru, which even the least sports-aware student at Reindeer Crescent knows she does every morning from six o'clock till the first bell rings.

My superfast sneakers shoot me through the early morning streets of Reindeer Crescent. These little nano-miracles on my feet are how I'm going to make human tornado Pru Quarles my instant best friend. With these sneakers, I'm as fast, if not faster, than her, which makes me a rival running machine. I play out the scenario in my head.

"Hey, you're the girl who broke Big Green," she'll say.

I won't respond. I'll just nod as I run alongside her and effortlessly keep pace.

She's going to be freaked out. How am I this fast? How does she not know about me? I'll shrug it off. "I don't have your focus," I'll tell her. "I just like to feel the wind in my hair."

She'll totally buy something like that and won't feel threatened by me at all. If anything, she'll want to mentor me. "You're a natural," she'll say. We'll spend more time running together. My casual attitude toward track will loosen her up. Meanwhile, I'll get a little of her ambition and determination. We'll be an odd couple but we'll be best friends.

I've envisaged a whole tears-and-triumph-filled future for me and Pru Quarles by the time I reach Reindeer Crescent's track. *She sprains her ankle just before the Olympics. Everything she's worked for, gone in a second. I step in, even though I've never run competitively, and win gold. "This is for you, Pru," I tell the world.*

There's an orchestra blaring in my head but, now that I'm looking around the track, there's no sign of Pru! *Don't say she's sprained her ankle for real?* Or worse: What if she's been approached already? What if I'm too late?

I hear the faint sound of someone running but there's

no one on the track. I whirl around. I see a figure open a door at the back of the school and disappear inside.

"Pru!" I yell.

My sneakers speed me to the door. It opens into the kitchen behind the cafeteria. I hear faint footsteps. I grab a hardened half bagel and take a bite. Bad decision. I remove the inedible bagel from my mouth, throw it into a white plastic trash can, and run through the cafeteria in search of the footsteps, which are getting fainter. I charge down the gym corridor past the space Big Green used to occupy. I think back fondly to our brief time together. I push open the double doors at the end of the gym corridor. I hear footsteps but I also hear a different kind of echo. Pru's taking the stairs. She's headed for the first floor.

Even with my fast and furious sneakers, I'm still nervous that I might slip on a stair and go down face-first. What if I lost a tooth? Maybe Spool could fit me with a nanotooth? But what would that do? I hear a classroom door slam and my thoughts snap back to the reason I'm here. I hit the top of the stairs, veer right, and follow the trail of locked classroom doors. Then I hit one that isn't locked. The window is open.

Pru?

I push open the door and walk through the empty room. When I get to the window, I see the fire escape ladder.

I hear footsteps from above.

She's climbing the shaky ladder that leads up onto the roof.

I could be eating cereal with my family right about now. But then I think about the averted eyes and long silences my presence would no doubt inspire and I feel a little more comfortable climbing out the window of an empty classroom and following a track star up a rusty ladder that sways and squeaks every time my foot hits a step.

I look up. No sign of Pru, which can only mean one thing for the Young Gazelle.

I'm going all the way up to the roof.

Immediately, I do *not* like the way the steps creak under my feet. I do *not* like how the whole ladder shakes as I make my way to the top. I do *not* like the way the rust has eaten its way through the ladder. If I move too fast or step too hard I feel like the whole thing will crumble to dust.

I climb carefully off the top step of the ancient ladder and land in the gravel that covers the roof of Reindeer

Crescent. I've never been up here. I've heard Ryan tell many, *many* stories about throwing firecrackers and old bicycles off the roof. I've heard Natalie talk about how the choir sometimes practices on the roof because being under the sky brings out a more emotional performance. And now here I am looking for the track star I hope to bamboozle into being my best friend so I can save her from being abducted by an enemy agency. The Wilder siblings, ladies and gentlemen, in all our many colors.

"Pru!" I call out again.

Nothing. Only my voice echoing back at me.

"Bridget?"

That was a man's voice.

I get tense. Where's Pru? Is this an enemy agent? I've only ever faced Doom Patrol and they pretty much fell to pieces when I kicked their hats off.

I hear the sound of footsteps on gravel a few yards away from me.

And Carter Strike walks out from behind a silver heating duct.

Same black leather jacket. Same serious look on his face.

"Agent . . . Carter . . . Dad . . . ," I babble.

"Where's the girl?"

"Pru? You know about her?" Of course he knows

about her. *She's on the radar.* "I followed her up here but she . . ." I don't want to tell him I lost her.

He nods. "They got her." I see him make a quick mental calculation. "We've got to move. You don't get airsick, do you?"

Yes. "No," I say.

"Good. There's a chopper on the way."

A chopper, as in helicopter?

"We'll get her back," he says, giving me a reassuring look.

I should tell him I've got school. I should tell him I need to check with my parents. I don't do any of these things. I'm getting on a chopper to save an abducted athlete from enemy agents with my superspy dad. Good luck with your boring day.

I hear the faint beating of helicopter blades getting louder.

Carter Strike beckons me toward the edge of the roof.

"Bridget, don't!" shouts a voice.

I see the chubby substitute teacher, Mr. B-or-D, coming off the top step of the ladder and hitting the roof. He's pretty fast for a heavyset guy. In fact, he's *really* fast. He comes barreling toward me.

"Get away from him," he shouts at me.

"It's all right," I tell him. "He's my father."

"No, he isn't," says Mr. B-or-D.

Carter Strike puts himself between me and the chubby substitute.

"He's just some guy from my school," I tell Strike. "He's not even a real teacher."

"I know who he is," says Agent Strike. He presses his palms together and gives the substitute a little bow. "You've no idea what an honor this is."

"Let her go," says the sub to my dad. "You don't need her. You've got me."

This has become very confusing.

"Wait, do you know each other?" I say, looking between the two of them.

"Bridget, walk away now," says Mr. B-or-D.

"But Pru?" I say.

"There is no Pru," says the sub.

"There is too a Pru," I say.

"She's not in any danger," says the sub. "Spool made it up to get you here."

"Next thing you'll be telling her there's no tooth fairy," says Agent Strike.

"Let her go," says the sub.

"As you wish," says Agent Strike. He raises his palms and takes a couple of steps away from me.

I'm not sure what's going on here but I don't like the

fact that I don't seem to have any say in it.

"What if I don't want to go?" I say. "I'm not some little schoolgirl."

Agent Strike smiles at the sub. "Admit it, we do good work." He puts an arm around my shoulders.

The substitute teacher lets out what sounds like a strangled yell of anger. He moves like lightning. With one hand, he pulls me away from Agent Strike; with the other, he grabs Agent Strike's wrist and twists it in ways hands are not meant to be twisted. The pain drops my dad to his knees.

"Stop it!" I yell. "You're hurting him."

My dad kicks out a leg and slams it straight into the sub's knee. He hooks a foot around the sub's ankle and topples him to the ground. As he falls, the sub grabs my dad and pulls him down with him. I'm not sure what's happening now but it looks like he spins around as he falls and crosses both legs around my dad's neck.

I am able to register what is happening in front of me but that is all. I am completely frozen to the spot. Even though I see my biological father and my substitute teacher fighting on the roof of my school, I might as well be watching it on TV. What's happening here in no way seems real.

Agent Strike's face gets redder and redder as he tries

to wriggle out of the sub's tight grip. But the chubby guy applies more pressure with his legs and my dad can't break the hold he's in.

"Bridget," Strike gasps. "Help."

It takes me a second to realize my father is asking for my help. I don't know what to do. Then I do. I pull out my lip balm, twist the bottom, and shove it in the substitute's face. Smoke billows out. He starts coughing. My dad breaks the grip. He pulls out a syringe and jabs it into the side of the sub's neck. All the fight leaves Mr. B-or-D's body.

As the awkward substitute drifts out of consciousness, he looks up at me and says, "Bridget, I'm your father."

"What?" I say. Then I feel a sharp pain in the side of my own neck and everything starts to go blurry.

CHAPTER TWENTY-NINE

Take Your Daughter to Work Day

Oh my God, I overslept. I'm going to be late for the algebra test I didn't study for. Once again, I'm letting everybody down. But it's not all my fault. I didn't hear Katy Perry. I didn't hear Dad blow his nose. I didn't hear Ryan breaking things. Why do my eyes feel so heavy? I never usually find it this hard to wake up. I stretch and yawn. Why is my bed so hard? My head is pounding. There's a nasty taste in my mouth. I keep swallowing but I can't get rid of it. With an effort, I push open my eyes. Everything's watery and out of focus. I feel like there's a memory lying just outside my reach that I can't quite get at. Something that will explain what happened to make me feel like this.

I hear a loud snore followed by a grunt. Am I not alone? Did Ryan sleep here last night? Did he tumble in and roll onto the floor like a dog?

"Ryan?" I try to say, but my mouth feels muddy and swollen.

"Bridget?" I hear a voice say my name. I'm *not* alone, but that is not Ryan. I try to turn onto my side to focus on the source of the voice but I can't move. I feel myself start to panic. I kick and struggle.

"Don't fight it," says the voice to my left.

I turn my head.

"Who are you? How did you get in my room?"

"We're not in your room, Bridget. I need you to try and stay calm. Concentrate on my voice. I want you to breathe slow, regular breaths. Relax. No one hurt you, and no one's *going* to hurt you."

The voice is calm and reassuring. I feel my panic subside. I squint my eyes a couple of times.

What was blurred starts to come into focus.

I can see the person to my left.

It's the substitute teacher, Mr. B-or-D. He's lying on a long metal table. His wrists and ankles are tied down with thick leather straps. The table that holds him is in the middle of an empty room with gleaming stainless steel walls and a big rectangular blacked-out window.

"What happened to you?" I ask. "What are you doing in here?"

As soon as I ask him those questions, it occurs to me that I'm in here, too. I'm lying on a metal table. My wrists and ankles are tied.

"Bridget, don't scream," says the sub.

I scream. I scream and thrash and pull at the straps. I keep screaming until my throat is raw. I struggle till the skin breaks on my wrists and ankles. I give up and let myself go limp.

"I'm sorry," says the substitute.

I fight for breath. "What are you talking about?"

"They wanted me and they went through you to get me."

"What did you do? What do I have to do with you? Why am I here?"

"I went so deep they couldn't find me, so they used the one thing they knew would bring me back on the grid."

I don't know what's worse, being tied to this table or being stuck with a substitute teacher who talks nonsense.

"Okay," I say. "Let me ask you something simple and you try to respond in a way that I can understand. Who are you?"

The sub says nothing for a second. "I'm your father," he suddenly blurts out. "Your real father."

I let out a laugh of disbelief. Even under the direst circumstances, Bridget Wilder still hangs on to her sense of humor.

"It's true," he insists.

"It's not true," I counter. "My real father is Carter Strike."

"I'm Carter Strike," he says.

"Right," I say. "So that other guy, the big tall guy in the leather jacket who calls himself Carter Strike, who's he? 'Cause it's not a common name. . . ."

"He was there to make you believe."

"Believe in what?"

"Believe you had a secret father who looked like a spy from the movies and wanted you to be a spy just like him."

My head is pounding worse than before. It's the sub's voice. He's so whiny and irritating.

"You're making this up," I say.

"But no real father would willingly put his child in danger. He'd want to protect her. And they knew that . . ."

"Who's *they*?"

"Section 23."

"Section 23, the famous government agency, the one that saves the world on a regular basis? They sent a guy to pretend to be Carter Strike so they could recruit me? Listen to what you're saying. Why would they do that?"

"Because they're the bad guys," he says without hesitation. "And I was a bad guy, too. Until I got out."

Everything I thought I knew starts slipping away.

"I don't believe you," I say. But the truth is, I don't know what I believe.

"They want what's in my head. All the secrets I took with me when I ran. They thought I was going to sell what I know to the highest bidder or use it against them. When they couldn't find me, they found . . ." He stops talking.

"Found who?"

"I knew they'd track her down. I knew they were going to go after everyone I'd ever known. I didn't know she'd had a daughter."

I want to be dreaming. I want to be dead asleep right now. I want to be anywhere other than in this steel room hearing what I'm hearing.

"Who had a daughter? Say it."

"Your mother," he says. "She was an agent with the Chechen secret service."

I try to sit up as much as I can given my restraints. Then I let myself fall and, as I do, I bang the back of my head as hard as I can on the metal table.

"Bridget, stop," he says.

I hear the concern in his voice, and I believe it is real. But I can't stop. I want to knock myself unconscious because I can't deal with what he's telling me. Could you? Could you handle being used and lied to on *this* scale? And then throw in a Eastern European spy mommy for good measure? I can't.

"Are you okay?" this man who claims he's my father asks.

I don't reply. I don't want to get into a conversation with him because the more he tells me, the more everything I think I know about myself is going to be stripped way. The more he tells me, the less special I'm going to be. I used to accept my invisibility. That was before Section 23. Before they made me feel like I was somebody. Before they used me. Now what am I? A moving part in someone else's plan. No superenhanced sneakers. No nanopowered black-and-gold tracksuit. No more Glasses of Truth. All the little accessories I loved so much. All gone. I must have been *so* hard to recruit. Spool must have had to fight the urge to laugh in my stupid gullible face. And what was the real Agent Carter Strike doing while I, his supposed daughter, was being puppeteered into betraying her friends and family?

"Why didn't you stop this?" I shout at him. "You saw me at school. You made a point of talking to me. Why didn't you protect me?"

Now it's Strike's turn to go quiet. "I don't trust anyone," he finally says. "It comes with the job. The longer you lie for a living, the less you believe anything anyone says. You hear rumors you've got a daughter, your immediate response is you're being lured into a trap."

I kick at the leather straps. "Good instinct. If only you'd acted on it, we might not be here."

"I know. I should have . . ." He trails off. "This life. Caring about someone else is a weakness your enemies can exploit. The first time I saw you, I think I knew it was true. But I convinced myself you were a plant. My thinking was, if I didn't acknowledge it, Section 23 would doubt their own intel. They'd start to think I had manipulated them . . ." He sighs. "This is what an old burned-out spy sounds like. I'm sorry, Bridget. I had hoped my first real conversation with my daughter wouldn't have been about how I disappointed her."

Something about the defeated way he talks is familiar to me. *He reminds me of me.* I'm not an old burned-out spy. I'm not any kind of spy. But I'm no stranger to disappointing others.

After a moment, I say, "So . . . how did you like being a substitute?"

He groans.

"What, worse than being a spy?"

"No one pays any attention and everyone's attached to their phones and no one knows anything and everyone speaks in those whiny, scratchy voices. And as for that kid Brendan Chew . . ."

"Lump, right?"

"Total lump," says Carter Strike.

And we laugh. Strapped down to metal tables in the middle of a stainless steel room, not knowing where we are or what's going to happen to us, Carter Strike and I laugh.

"This family bond between you is a beautiful thing to see," says the echoey voice suddenly filling the room.

"Here we go," whispers Carter Strike.

I lift my head as far as I can and see the big rectangular window is no longer black. It looks into a cramped little office with a small wooden desk dominated by a huge laptop. Behind the desk sits a pink-faced man.

"Spool," I say.

"Spool," says Strike, at exactly the same time.

Spool breaks into a wide grin. "You two are adorable."

He gets up from the desk and walks to the window. I was hoping he might be a disembodied head that would float away like an untethered balloon. But no. The head is attached to an ordinary, mildly flabby body wearing a gray suit.

"Let her go, Spool," says Strike. "You don't need her. You've got me. I'll cooperate *if* she walks free."

Spool smiles. "That would be crazy. She's my leverage. I'm not letting her walk away."

Clunk. The final piece of the puzzle entitled *Let's Betray Bridget* falls into place.

Spool sees it. He sees that I get it. I get how he used me. I hope he sees the hate in my face.

"Come on, don't be mad," he says. "I didn't tell the whole truth, but I made your life better."

"Better?" I yell. "I've alienated my family. My friends. Everyone at school. You've made me more of an outcast than I ever was."

"Look at it this way," he says. "If it hadn't been you, it would have been another girl. You saved someone's life. That's a good thing."

"What? What other girl? I don't know what you're talking about."

"Tell her, Dad," says Spool.

I twist around on the table until I can see Strike. He

looks more uncomfortable than I've ever seen him.

"The reason I didn't believe you were my daughter is . . . you weren't the first."

I'm confused. "First what?"

"The first daughter Spool used as bait."

"You've got another daughter?"

"No," says Strike. "You're the only one. They found you before I did."

"What happened to the other girl?" I ask.

"Girls," says Spool. "They couldn't fool Strike. They were no use to anyone."

I want to ask again what happened to them. But I don't want to know the answer.

"Think, Spool," I yell. "I've got a family. I matter to people. They're going to notice I'm missing."

Spool leans back against his desk, looking smug. "That's where you're wrong. We've cloned you down to the last detail. The clone has moved into your home and your family already like it better than you."

"No!" I shout. "They wouldn't fall for that. They'd know the difference."

But even while I'm yelling at Spool, I'm thinking, *Would I know the difference? If someone replaced Ryan or Natalie with a clone, would I even notice? And they've got big personalities. They're not halfway invisible, like I was. Oh my God.*

"They didn't clone you," says Strike. "Section 23 are notorious cheapskates and this operation has stretched their budget to its breaking point. They splurged on a whole Smart Car."

"Our budget got a lot bigger since we sold Nick Deck's secrets to the highest bidder, and we're getting a lot of interest in these missile codes," says Spool.

"You're going to start a war," yells Strike.

"Couple of wars, probably," says Spool. "Good for business." He grins at me. "We could absolutely clone you if we wanted to. We haven't *yet*. But we're not going to let you go. You're a talented little spy, Bridget Wilder. . . ."

"No. No way," barks Strike. "Don't do it."

"Don't do what?" I ask.

"Yes, don't do what?" asks Spool. "Don't plant triggers into her subconscious that, when activated, turn her into the perfect Section 23 agent and then wipe what she just did from her memory? That the sort of thing you don't want us to do?"

"I'll come back to work for you," says Strike. "I'll do anything you say, without question."

I squirm around on the table to watch his face while

he's saying this. His eyes are wide. He nods his head as he speaks. He looks scared to death.

"Why would I want an old burned-out spy?" grins Spool. "When our new breed of agent has worked out so well?"

"What new breed?" says Strike.

A panel in the stainless steel wall slides open. Dale Tookey walks in.

"I'm the new breed," he says. He flashes me a friendly smile. "How's the neck, Bridget? Sorry I had to jab you, but *now* we're even."

CHAPTER THIRTY

What Doesn't Kill You Makes You Stronger

Of course. Of course he had to be a spy. If he wasn't, I might have had one thing left: the fantasy that a boy liked me. So, of course, they had to take that away from me, too.

Dale Tookey looks a little apologetic. "I know this is weird."

"You don't talk to her," snarls Strike. "You don't even look at her."

"Sir, I get that you're upset and I completely understand where you're coming from, but I just want to say, Bridget, your daughter, she's really something. If you could see her out in the field. She shows no fear."

I liked him a whole lot better when he wasn't trying so hard.

"You heard the man," I all but spit. "Don't talk to me."

"I just want you to know that what's about to happen to you will be quick and painless."

"Unlike having to listen to you," I say.

Tookey nods. "The process of inserting the chip involves . . ."

"Boring me to death?" I interrupt.

"Ha!" snorts Strike. I like that I can make him laugh.

Tookey looks unimpressed. "Say your good-byes."

"No," says Strike. "We're not going anywhere."

"Beg to differ," says Tookey.

The stainless steel panel slides open again. The guy in the leather jacket walks in. The man who pretended to be my father.

"Rolf," says Tookey to the fake Strike.

The guy, who I guess is called Rolf, walks to the head of my metal table and begins to roll me out of the room.

Strike struggles on his table. I feel our hands touch briefly as my table passes his. Or maybe I just want to think that we made contact.

"Don't be scared, Bridget," he says, and his voice is

shaking. "I'm going to find you."

"I know you will," I say. "You're Carter Strike."

The guy called Rolf pushes my table out through the panel in the wall. I squirm around to try and look back at my real father. It starts to hit me. We had no time together.

"I'd love to go to Brazil! São Paulo," I shout back at him. "I like eating octopus—I like how rubbery it is. I hate horseflies."

"The size of them!" he calls after me.

The panel slides shut.

"Find me," I call. "Or I'll find you."

"Awww," says Rolf.

I lift my chin as high as I can to see his upside-down face. "I'm so glad you're not my father."

"Mutual," he says.

Rolf continues to push me and my metal table down a long brightly lit corridor. Dale Tookey walks beside me, studying his phone and shooting me sidelong looks.

"You okay?" he asks. "You doing okay?"

"Thank you so much for asking," I say, as frostily as I can manage, which, under the circumstances, is *quite* frosty. "I'm having a lovely time. I'll remember it always. Oh wait, no I won't. 'Cause you're about to slice my brain open and shove a chip in it."

"Can't wait till that happens. Maybe it'll shut her up," says Rolf.

"You're perfect father material, Rolf," I say. "No way your kids are going to be scarred for life."

"That's right, keep talking," Rolf replies.

"Leave her alone," says Tookey.

"There's my knight in shining armor," I say. "My backstabbing knight in shining garbage."

"Bridget," he starts to say. Then he stops. I feel his hand touch the strap around my left wrist.

"Rolf, wait."

"They want her in there," says Rolf. "The process."

"Look at her wrists, man. They're raw. Same with her ankles."

"Good. Hope it hurts," says my phony dad.

"What if the pain keeps her alert through the process, helps her fight it?"

"That's not our call."

"I'll tell Spool you said that."

Rolf sucks his teeth in annoyance. He stops pushing the table.

"Untie her ankles. I'll get her wrists," says Tookey.

"I don't think so," grumbles Rolf. "What if she . . . ?"

"She's a scared little schoolgirl," Tookey interrupts. "You're a brick wall."

Rolf stomps down to the end of the table and starts tugging at the straps around my ankles.

Tookey goes to my left hand. He undoes the strap with one hand. With his other hand, he begins stroking my palm.

"Get your hands off me," I snarl.

He keeps stroking it. Tracing his finger up and down and around my palm. I realize what he's doing. Tookey's not caressing my hand. He's spelling something. I concentrate on the movement of his finger on my palm.

D-I-E.

He's telling me he's going to kill me.

Tookey goes to my right side, undoes the strap.

Down at the bottom of the table, Rolf is taking his time freeing me, making sure he causes maximum pain.

Tookey looks at Rolf bent over my ankle. I see him pull something from inside his jacket pocket. It's a syringe.

He's going to do it now. I'm dead.

Unless . . .

Rolf frees my ankles. I spring up onto the table. I kick the syringe out of Tookey's hand and catch it. In one fluid motion, I hurl it straight back at him. It catches him in the shoulder. He gasps, claws at the syringe, and then folds up and slumps to the ground.

Rolf growls and makes a grab at me. I jump into the

air, high as I can. When I fall back to the table, I stamp my foot down hard on Rolf's outstretched hand. I imagine I hear bones crack. I like that sound. So much so that I spin around and kick out behind me. My heel catches Rolf square on his handsome nose. I *definitely* heard something crack that time.

Rolf has both hands covering his gushing nose. I use this opportunity to leap upward one more time. When I come down, I drive my knees into the back of Rolf's head, forcing it down onto the metal table.

"Mutual, Rolf!" I scream.

He hits the ground with a thud. I remain standing on the metal table, breathless, shaking, adrenaline coursing through my veins. I look down at the two motionless bodies on the ground. I did that.

Wait, *I* did that? No speedy shoes, no nano-tracksuit? But then it occurs to me. I've been running incredible distances at amazing speeds these past few weeks. Spool's gadgets may have transported me, but it was my legs and my body that were moving. I didn't anticipate this byproduct, and I know Section 23 didn't, but . . .

I'm ripped.

I let out a low chuckle and savor my unexpected power.

Then Spool and a bunch of Section 23 agents burst

out of the far door at the end of the corridor. Another load of agents pour through a door at the opposite end.

I can take them, I think for approximately one second.

I decide retreat is my best and only option. I squat down low and then spring up, pushing myself as high as I can. I punch two fists in the air and knock out a ceiling panel directly above me. I reach skyward, grab both ends of the panel, and pull myself up.

I feel a hand grab at my ankle. The fingernails dig in where the flesh is at its most tender. I grit my teeth and hold in my cry of pain. I grope around inside the exposed ceiling area for something, anything, to use as a weapon, to break the hold around my ankle, which is getting increasingly painful and harder to resist.

My hand touches something soft and hairy. Whatever's up there is gross enough to make me momentarily forget the grip on my ankle. I grab the fleshy thing and throw it at the owner of the hand on my leg. I glance downward. It's a rat. I had a dead rat in my hand.

Groooooooossssss!

I shudder in horror. But the hand lets go of my ankle.

Beneath me, I hear a loud male scream of horror.

"It's biting me!"

Oh my God! It wasn't a dead rat. I had a live rat in my hand. And that live rat just saved my life, so I instantly resolve to be more caring toward all rats living and dead from now on. (I'm pretty sure I'm going to break that resolution.)

The agent beneath me keeps screaming. I haul myself up through the panel and find myself in a tight and constricted air vent.

I'm a little bit claustrophobic and, as I've just discovered, this particular confined space is a favored hangout for live rats. But there's no other way for me to go but forward, so I squeeze my elbows out and start crawling into the unknown.

CHAPTER THIRTY-ONE

Vent

"Not smart, Bridget," Spool's voice shouts up from the corridor beneath me.

"That's what they call me," I reply. Not the most hilarious comeback, maybe, but the best I can manage in my current situation.

"I've read your psychological evaluation," I hear him say. "I know you don't respond well to being confined in small spaces. The panic's about to set in. You can feel it, can't you? It's getting harder to breathe. Your heart is racing."

"I know what you're trying to do," I say. "But you're

talking about someone who doesn't exist anymore."

He doesn't reply. I know I've made him think. I can imagine his little pink brain throbbing and pulsing. What if I've become an unpredictable wild card? Someone whose every reaction he can't anticipate? What if by manipulating me he's accidentally made me into someone he can no longer manipulate? That's what I'm hoping he's thinking. In fact, he's not wrong about me being stuck up in this air vent. I'm on the verge of freaking out. I can't catch my breath, my heart is pounding in my ears, and what little space there is seems to be closing in around me. My elbows bang against the sides of the vent. My head touches the ceiling. Back down there, in that corridor, on that table, I was so strong. I felt like I could do anything. Up here, in this vent, I'm nothing. I can barely crawl. I feel the strain in my elbows and my shoulders. I'm using everything I've got to drag myself forward but I'm hardly moving. I don't know how long I've been up here. It could be minutes. It could be hours. But I've made next to no progress. Maybe that's why Spool's gone so quiet. Maybe he's letting me die up here. I wish I hadn't just thought that because now I can't think about anything else. This is what it's like to be buried alive. No one to hear you. No one to help you.

Walled in. No energy left to breathe, let alone scream. Completely alone.

Except I'm not alone.

It starts quietly. The little pitter-patter of tiny feet on metal. Then it gets louder. Something's in here with me. And it's getting closer. Obviously I know what it is. But I've never, ever wanted so much to be wrong.

Here it comes. Scampering into view. Tiny black eyes getting me in their sights. There's no way I'm not going to pee all over myself. But why? This rat doesn't know me. I haven't given this rat any reason to fear me. Circumstances have stuck us both up in this vent. There's no reason we can't peacefully coexist.

"Hi, Ratty," I breathe. "Hey, buddy. Don't worry, I'm not invading your territory. Just passing through. How about you turn back and let me go on my way."

The rat rears up at the sound of my voice. I think I just gave it a reason to fear me. He—I'm saying he, maybe it's a she, I can't tell—breaks into a ratlike gallop. His moist, bulging, hairy rat body undulates as he moves. I see his eyes, his twitching snout, his nasty little teeth. I push my elbows against the sides of the vent and try to back up. But it's like I'm swimming through cement and the rat is gliding through the air. He's getting closer. I don't have the strength to scream. I squeeze my eyes shut.

And then I hear a loud bang.

I open an eye in time to see the rat explode in a burst of blood and rodent flesh.

Ewww.

Please tell me none of that got on my face.

"Warning shot, Bridget," Spool's voice calls up. "Next one's going to hurt."

If I had the strength to laugh, I'd be yukking it up in my rat-splattered vent home.

"You're important to me but not so important that I won't hurt you if I have to."

"Same here," I say, full of false bravado. "Except for the important part."

"Shoot her in the thigh," I hear him say.

I try to think like a spy. Is he bluffing? How much use could I really be to him on crutches? His credibility as a brilliant leader must have taken a bit of a dip with me escaping and wiping the floor with two trusted henchmen. Maybe I matter less than his standing in the eyes of his agents. Perhaps it would be smart to engage in a bit of pleading and groveling. That way I avoid pain and live to fight another day.

"Don't shoot," I start to say.

I don't think anyone's listening. I think something's

happening down there. I hear a sudden commotion. Shouts. The sound of a scuffle. Punches being exchanged. Screams. A loud thump. Then another. And another. Footsteps hit the ground, running out of earshot. And silence.

"Bridget?" That voice sounds familiar. "It's me. It's your fa . . . it's Agent . . . it's Strike."

He's got the same problem as me. What do I call him?

"Strike? You escaped. I did, too. I beat up two agents."

"You did? That's fantastic. I'm so proud of you."

"Are you okay? There were a lot of bad guys down there."

"Less now."

"You've got amazing moves for a guy your size." I wince as soon as I say that. "Sorry, I didn't mean . . ."

"It's fine. I've got a pyroid problem. It's like a thyroid problem, except it involves eating pies."

He's kind of corny. But I have no problem with that.

"Maybe you can show me some of your techniques," I say.

"It's a date. Now let's get you down from there."

I start to back up. The footsteps that ran out of earshot suddenly come charging back.

"New plan!" yells Strike. "They sent in reinforcements. Get out of here. Go as fast as you can. Head upward. I'll meet you once I'm done here."

The shouting and scuffling resumes below.

I'm newly motivated and fully energized. I start to crawl forward. My limbs no longer feel like they weigh a ton. I no longer fear ending up entombed in the air vent. I can breathe. My heart rate is under control. My only immediate problem is that I have to negotiate my way past what remains of my buddy the rat. There's not much left of him but what there is, is red and sticky. I close my eyes, hold my breath, crawl forward, and . . .

Groooooosssss!

Freedom. Escaping Spool. Reuniting with my family. Working out the logistics of my relationship with Strike. None of these things are making me move so fast through this vent as the prospect of a hot shower that lasts for thirteen weeks. I'm beating the heck out my elbows and knees but it's going to be worth it. Once I'm past Rat-Remains Junction, I'm a vent-crawling machine. I squeeze around a corner, drag my aching bones along a widening passage of vent, and there directly ahead of me is a sight so beautiful it should be accompanied by a swelling of violins and a heavenly choir. It's the light at the end of the tunnel. Or, in my case—and much more important—it's the grille at the end of the vent.

Obviously, me being me, what-ifs start to fill my

head. What if the grille is screwed tightly into the surrounding wall? What if it's locked and the lock can only be opened from the outside? What if the grille ultimately leads nowhere? What if all that's on the other side is wall?

Uh-uh. No way. I beat Rolf. I beat rat. I'm not being beaten by grille. I power forward till I'm close enough to see that the worst of my fears was unfounded. There is something on the other side of the grille. A little burst of white that compels me on. I drag myself forward till my nose is inches away from the metal panel. This is going to take deep reserves of strength. This is going to take me being patient and consistent. I'm prepared to work away at the grille until my fingers are bloody stubs, until it becomes as natural an act to me as breathing, until I'm free.

I work my arms under my chest and then shove them forward to test the level of grille resistance I'll need to deal with. My palms touch the metal and . . . the grille falls away from the wall. I'm almost disappointed. Almost.

I squeeze myself out. Drag myself to my feet and attempt to brush the dirt, blood, and bits of rat carcass from my T-shirt. I squint a couple of times and try to adjust my eyes to the blinding all-encompassing whiteness surrounding me. I wonder what godforsaken corner of Section 23 I've wound up in. What sort of deadly secret stuff is carried out inside all this whiteness.

"Hello, darling," trills a warm, familiar voice. "My favorite customer's back."

"Xan with an X?" I say.

"So nice to see you again. And look who's here. My *other* favorite customer."

I follow Xan's right arm and see that her long tapering fingers and beautifully manicured nails are digging into the neck of my tearful, terrified, confused, angry friend Joanna.

CHAPTER THIRTY-TWO

Xan with an X. The blindingly white room. Joanna. Brain goes *click click click*. I'm in the mall. The Reindeer Crescent mall! I'm in what was once IMAGE UNLTD, the superposh clothes store that mysteriously sent me a gift card for my birthday. A gift card I thought Joanna had sent me. Which, to her mind, must have been the start of increasingly bizarre behavior on my part. So she's been furtively sneaking around, trying to piece together the truth about my transformation. Which led her to this big white empty store. IMAGE UNLTD doesn't exist anymore. But what's underneath does: Section 23's supersecret headquarters.

Xan with an X spotted Joanna lurking around and discovered the perfect hostage to use against me. Brain exhausted.

"What's the plan, Xan?" I say, cool as I can muster.

"Block the flow of blood from lovely Joanna's brain if you don't do what I say," she replies, her perfect features calm and clear like a pool of water. Xan removes her hand from Joanna's neck. Joanna doesn't move. Fear has frozen her to the spot.

"If I made it up here, you must realize I left a trail of broken Section 23 bodies behind me," I say. "Don't make me add you to the list."

Xan lets out a laugh like the tinkling of tiny bells. "Look at you, you spy diva. You're so different from the scared little mouse who crept in here weeks ago." She makes tiny trembling mouse fingers to illustrate her point that I was timid and twitchy.

"Rolf looks like a broken jigsaw," I tell her. "I'd hate to have to rearrange that pretty face of yours."

Xan sighs and clasps her hands. She gives me this big soulful wide-eyed look that, I can't lie, makes me melt. "I am so proud right now I could cry. I really could. I look at you and I think, I made her. I taught her to walk or, in your case, run. I gave you strength. And now you've come to challenge me, to assert your independence, which is the most natural thing in the world."

The soothing tone of her voice, her steady gaze: Xan's having a hypnotic effect on me.

"Spool's got no social skills. He doesn't know how to put people at ease. Listen to me, I've got your best interests at heart. You need Section 23 and we need you. Come back downstairs with me, Bridget. Get the chip. The process is quick and painless. You're already amazing."

She's lulling me. I'm definitely being lulled.

Then she says, "You already make me feel like a proud mother. Make me even prouder."

This un-lulls me. It un-lulls the *crap* out of me.

I've already got a mother. In fact, it turns out I've got two. I don't need this one.

"You're not my mother, you're my Frankenstein," I say.

"I'll take it." She shrugs. "He was a doctor."

"And he was killed by his monster," I say.

"You realize you're calling yourself a monster," chimes in Joanna.

Xan and I both look startled. We'd forgotten she was there.

"So you're talking to me now?" I say.

"What, you're so hard up for friends you have to get your paid muscle to threaten me? Pretty pathetic."

"You're the pathetic one if anyone's pathetic. What are you doing here, Joanna? You hate the mall. But you wanted to find out something about me, right? Dig up something juicy."

"Right. Because everyone's *so* interested in Bridget Wilder and her exciting life."

"You keep writing about my exciting life in your Tumblr!"

"It's a group text. I have a hundred and twenty-five followers."

"That's down from before."

"It's plateaued. The real hardcore fans stuck with me."

"That's great, Joanna. So you don't need any *real* friends."

"You were never my friend."

I gasp at this. "I *tried*. You know how hard it is being friends with you? How mean you are? The way you resent everybody."

"I always knew you were waiting for someone better," Joanna says. "I was just the substitute until Casey Breakbush rolled her window down and gave you the golden ticket."

"I said I was sorry about that."

"You never said you were sorry."

I think she might be right.

"I'm sorry, okay? I didn't want to."

"Don't think you can come groveling back to me. I don't need you."

"I wasn't about to grovel."

"Good. 'Cause I don't care about you and whatever nitwit thing you're doing here."

"Ladies, please, this is exhausting," says Xan. "You're both beautiful, strong, intelligent young women. Now more than ever, we need to support each other, not tear each other down."

"Excuse me?" I say. "You want to kill her and turn me into a zombie."

"We can still respect each other," says Xan.

"You think I respect you? You're everything I never want to be." I start counting on my fingers. "Traitor. Coward. Lackey. Liar. Awesome job you got here, Xan with an X. Spool starts wars. You pretend to sell shoes. He must have a ton of faith in you."

Unflattering splotches of red appear on Xan's face. "You're a stupid little girl. You don't know anything."

"I am a little girl." I nod. "But I'm an awesome spy, you said as much. And I'm just going to get better as I get older. From what I've seen of Section 23, there's only room for one queen bee. Spool's desperate to keep me around. But you . . ."

I look at my watch. "Time's ticking away," I say, in case the point wasn't clear.

"She's totally had work done," says Joanna. "If you stand where I'm standing, you can see the marks behind the ears."

"Stop it," Xan screeches. She stabs her nail back into Joanna's neck. Joanna moans in pain. Xan smiles at me. While she has Joanna by her side, she has power over both of us.

But we have power, too.

"You're right, Xan," I say. "We shouldn't be attacking each other. We should be looking out for each other. We're not the bad guys here."

I stare straight at Joanna. "Write this in the Conquest Report. It's time to *bite* the hand that feeds!"

I nod frantically at Joanna as I say this. For what is probably the first time in the history of our turbulent friendship, she listens to what I say.

Joanna grabs Xan's hand from her neck and sinks her teeth deep into the flesh.

Xan lets out a high-pitched shriek of surprise and pain. And I've been to a barbecue with Joanna; I've seen her go to town on a corncob. She leaves no man standing. Xan draws back her other hand to punch Joanna in the face. I charge at her. I jump on top of Joanna's shoulders. Xan goes to grab my leg. Too slow, ma'am. I spring straight up in the air and, as I come down, kick out a leg and wrap it around Xan's throat. I let myself fall backward to the ground, dragging her downward as I plummet. *Airborne Gazelle Stance!*

Xan flails and writhes, trying to remove me from around her neck. She slashes her arms at me. A punch catches me on the side of my head, making my ears ring. I've got the element of unpredictability on my side, but there's no way I'm going to be able to hold her long enough to choke her out.

"Bridget!" Joanna yells. "Move!"

I look up. Joanna stands a few inches from me. She sticks out her butt and aims it at the exact spot on Xan's face covered by my leg. I gasp in shock. Can she really be about to do this? I lift my leg and hurl myself away from Xan's gasping, bucking body. Her face is free for a second. Then a shadow falls over it. Then Joanna's butt falls over it. Xan continues to thrash and punch the air. I sit on Xan's stomach and use my knees to pin her wrists to the ground.

Muffled howls of rage are just about audible from

beneath Joanna's butt. Xan is not giving up without a fight.

I look over at Joanna. She winces in pain. I'm guessing Xan bit her.

I hold out my palm. Joanna looks at it. Then slaps it.

"You're amazing," I say, meaning it.

"You're a jerk," she says. "You could have told me."

"I . . . ," I start to say.

"You could have told me *something*," she says, her voice shaky. "You could have let me know it wasn't me, that you weren't abandoning me. That something big had happened to you."

"You'd have understood?"

"Of course not. I don't understand *now*. I don't even know who I'm sitting on. But you're including me."

I honest to God feel like tearing up. I can never tell Joanna everything. She would totally sell me out to her hundred and twenty-five followers. Then I'd have to see if Carter Strike could pull the right strings to get her and Big Log deported to Botswana. There's an ocean of lies and distrust between us. But right now, we've never been better friends.

"She's stopped," says Joanna.

No more muffled howls or thrashing come from Xan.

Now I'm scared we might have subdued her a little too well. With an effort, Joanna pushes herself up from Xan's face. I clamber off her arms. We look down at her still body. The pockets of Joanna's jeans have left red, ridged imprints on Xan's cheeks.

"I think you killed her," says Joanna.

"Me?" I squeak. "I held her arms. You suffocated her."

"Right. 'Cause my butt is so huge."

Xan's little bow mouth opens slightly; a low moan escapes. Her chest rises and falls. Joanna looks at me, relieved.

"Bridget?"

I know that voice. Carter Strike. He defeated the bad guys and made a clean getaway. He said he'd find me and he has.

"I want you to meet someone," I tell Joanna.

I turn to see my biological father's head, neck, and arms sticking out of the grille. The rest of him seems to be still inside.

"Little help here?"

"Isn't that the fat sub with the sweaty pits?" says Joanna. "What's he doing here?"

I give her an embarrassed grin and go to help yank Agent Carter Strike out of the air vent.

He suddenly yells, "Watch out!"

I look back to see Joanna splayed out unconscious on the ground. Xan kicks me in the stomach. Hard. I go flying across the blindingly white room. By the time I've recovered enough to get up, her foot is on my throat, forcing me back down. I can't breathe. I'm blacking out. I hear Strike's voice yelling my name, over and over.

"Thank you for shopping at IMAGE UNLTD," Xan says. "I look forward to serving you in the future. Or not."

I hear a roaring in my ears.

I hear the sound of glass shattering. It must be happening a million miles away.

I hear Carter Strike's voice. "Bridget, get out of the way! Roll over! Move!"

I can't imagine I have the strength to do what he's saying. But I try.

I sway from side to side but I can't quite get enough momentum to escape Xan's foot.

I feel two hands grab me and drag me away. I see a little red and white car reverse into Xan and pin her to the empty white wall.

I look at the very tall, very beautiful woman flapping helplessly under the weight of the Smart Car, whose door hangs open.

"Are you okay? Can you hear me? Do you know where you are?" The guy who drove the car, who jumped out at the last minute, who pulled me from under Xan's foot, who holds me in his arms—I can't quite focus, but it looks like Dale Tookey.

CHAPTER THIRTY-THREE

Blaze of Glory

I squirm out of Tookey's arms, push him away from me, and hit a fighting stance. He holds up both palms.

"I'm on your side."

"I've heard that before," I say.

"He's on our side," shouts Strike. "He's our man on the inside."

"He wrote D-I-E on my palm with his finger."

"That was L-I-E," says Tookey. "Like, all this is a lie and I'm on your side?"

"Oh. Well, that wasn't clear. Your finger technique needs work."

"I'm a double agent," Tookey says. "Maybe even triple. I'm never sure. Strike had me look out for you at school when he wasn't around."

"And pretend to like me," I say.

"I'm not that good a spy," he says. And then he looks embarrassed. "I'm an awesome hacker, though. I totally rebooted your tiny car. I used a command prompt that . . ."

"How's the shoulder?" I ask, making it plain that I'm trying to change the subject. "Sorry I had to jab you."

I hear a groan. Joanna. She's okay. Good. I should go over to her, make sure nothing's broken. But somehow I feel it's more important right at this minute to stay standing close to Dale Tookey.

"Break it up, you two lovebirds, I'm still stuck here!"

Dale and I hurry over to the grille, where we each grab a Strike arm.

"Did we do it?" I ask. "Did we actually beat Section 23?"

Dale looks down at Strike's face. "Boss?"

"We almost beat them."

I stop pulling Strike's arm. "What do you mean almost? Are they like ants? You cut off the head, they keep coming?"

Strike grimaces. "We didn't exactly cut off the head. The pink head."

I feel my stomach lurch. "Spool? He got away?"

"He's slippery," says Strike.

"We'll get him," says Dale.

"But we don't have him now," I say. "He's out there and . . ." Bye-bye, normal-Bridget brain. Welcome back, trust-no-one brain. Where would Spool go? What would he want right now? To save himself? My trust-no-one brain digs deeper. It thinks, *Spool decided he wants to recruit me and he will find some way to bend me to his will. Or somebody.*

"Leverage!" I yelp.

"What?" say Strike and Dale.

"Spool always has to have leverage. That's how he functions. That's how he manipulates. And his only leverage over me right now is . . ."

Oh my God. It's my family.

I grab Dale's phone, jump into the car, and slam the door. I glance in the rearview mirror and see Xan is still pinned against the wall. I bet that hurts.

"Bridget, wait," he says. He comes after me.

"Stop her!" yells Strike.

"You can't do this by yourself," I hear Dale yell. But I'm already in the car.

"Let's go," I tell the car.

"I don't work for you," says the car with my voice.

"Don't start with me, car," I bawl, thumping the dashboard for emphasis. "Spool's going after my family to get me back in line."

"Oh sure, it's all about you," mocks the car.

The engine starts. The car backs away from the store wall. Xan's body falls onto the hood and then plops onto the ground. Dale rushes after the car. He yanks the passenger door open. "I'm coming with you."

"Oooohhh," says the car in an annoying singsong voice. "What an incredible spontaneous romantic gesture."

"Shut up," Dale and I both tell the car.

The car reverses out of the broken IMAGE UNLTD store windows. A bunch of mall security guards have gathered outside and signal us to stop. We do not stop. The Smart Car maneuvers its way past confused mall shoppers and into the street.

"Change the license plate and the paint job," Dale orders the car.

I pick up Dale's phone and start to make a call. He takes the phone from my hand.

"Hey! I'm trying to call my mom."

Dale touches the screen. "I turned on the voice-masking app. We're about to be involved in a high-speed chase. She doesn't need to know it's you."

I give Dale a sidelong glance. He's very considerate. I hear my mom answer the phone.

"Mom . . . ," I begin, trying to keep the tremble out of my voice.

"She hears a man speaking, nitwit," says the car.

"Oh. Right. Mrs. Wilder? This is Inspector . . . um . . . Carr, from the Sacramento Police Department. I need you to stay where you are. Don't answer the door unless you see ID. Call Dad, um, Mr. Wilder, and tell him the same. Police. ID."

"Who is this?" my mom asks. "What's this about?"

"Please, Mrs. Wilder, it's important you do exactly as I say. It might be a false alarm but better safe than sorry. That's what we're telling the community. Where's your son, Ryan?"

"He left me some sort of message. I think he said he was spending the day at the Russian steam baths."

"And you're okay with this? He's not getting grounded? He just gets to do whatever he wants?"

"Stick to the story, Inspector," says Dale.

I try to calm down and sound official. "We've already been in contact with your daughter, Bridget, and she's safe. She's with her friend."

"Bridget's safe?" Mom echoes. "That's good. I worry about her."

"You don't need to worry. She's a strong, smart, sensible girl," I find myself saying.

"Sounds like you know her better than me," says Mom. "She just hit that age . . . everything I say or do is wrong."

This makes me feel horrible.

"I'm sure that's not true," I say. "She's under a lot of stress right now . . ."

"Really?" says Mom. "She told you that? What sort of stress. What else did she tell you?"

"Tell her it's a boy so you can move on," suggests Dale.

Without thinking, I say, "It's possible I like a boy."

"Okay," says my mother. "But what's that got to do with Bridget?"

I hear the car hoot with laughter.

"What about your other daughter, Mrs. Wilder? Where's Natalie?"

"She tutors special children after school today . . . oh wait . . ."

There's a silence on the other end of the line. Then Mom says, "I got a text from her. A theater producer saw a clip of her school musical on YouTube. He wants to talk to her about a show. Good things just happen to that girl."

Good things do happen to Natalie. But not this time. My spy senses just kicked in. And they kicked hard.

"What producer? What's his name? Where's he based? What's his contact number? Where's he meeting her?"

"Um . . . ," my mom says.

"Spool!" I shriek.

"What?"

"He's got my sister," I tell Dale.

"We'll get her back," he says. He starts tapping at a tablet. "I can trace the location of his texts. He thinks he's covered his tracks so well no one can follow them. He doesn't know about my advanced hacking skills. I'm fluent in a special version of SQL that reverses . . ."

Dale stops talking and looks at the panic on my face. "We'll get him."

He goes back to his tapping.

"Inspector?" I hear my mom's voice.

"I've got to go, ma'am. Stay safe. Do what I say. I love you. That is, the police love you. And the entire community."

I end the call and feel myself go limp. Not Natalie.

"This is my fault," I whisper. "I put her in danger."

"Stop," says Dale. "You're the victim here. Spool

used you. But you fought back. You turned his plan upside down."

"If he hurts her. If he plays with her head . . ." I can't bear the thought of Natalie in his clutches.

"I hate him," says the car. "She's such a better sister than you."

"I know." She's potentially a much better spy than me, too. I'm fairly confident Spool does not know this about Natalie. But what if he finds out? What if he tries to use her the way he used me?

"No!" I say out loud.

"Got him!" says Dale.

He logs Spool's coordinates into the Smart Car's GPS.

The Smart Car roars through Reindeer Crescent and turns onto the freeway. I gnaw on the skin at the top of my fingers, an unpleasant childhood habit I thought I was long beyond. But I need to concentrate on something; otherwise I'm going to have a massive meltdown in this tiny car.

Little snippets of songs start playing on the radio. So fast I barely recognize them. Dale must be skipping satellite stations.

"Can you stop that?" I say.

"It's not me," he says.

The stations keep skipping until they stop at "Who Wants to Live Forever" by Queen. The song plays in full.

"I thought it might make you feel better," says the car, minus its usual sarcasm.

"Car!" I say, touched.

"She learned it on her flute," the car tells Dale. "Still like her?"

"It was a phase," I assure him. "I'm sure you had worse ones."

He starts to smile at me but the smile fades. "Only if it was for an assignment. Only if it was part of my cover. Section 23 got me young. I was a runaway. Being a spy is all I know."

"But Strike got you out."

"He got me another side to spy for. I'm not a real person, Bridget. I'm a collection of bits of people I've pretended to be." Dale leans in close to me. "And you'll be just like me unless you get out now. Once this is over. Once we get your sister back. Stop. Don't let Strike keep you in play."

"He wouldn't do that. He wants me safe."

"He *wants to* want to keep you safe. He wants to be a good guy but he was a bad guy a lot, *lot* longer."

"Are you saying I can't trust him?"

"I'm saying you may be his daughter but you're also an awesome asset."

I know Dale thinks he's looking out for me but he's making me feel very alone. "The only people in the world I can trust are my family and I've put them all in harm's way. You don't have to worry about me. I'm going to go back to being the ordinary, invisible girl I used to be."

Am I? Is that what I really want?

"I can't wait," I say with as much conviction as I can muster.

Dale nods.

"And you can walk away, too," I tell him.

He gives me a pained look. His tablet emits a loud *beep!*

"Spool's vehicle approximately one thousand yards ahead," says the car.

"Floor it, car," I say.

"That's not the move," says Dale. "We hang back, stay out of sight, follow him, see where he's going, see if he's got a safe house set up."

I shake my head vigorously. "I want her out of there now!"

"Listen to me," Dale says, and I can see he's trying to stay calm. "We'll get Natalie and we'll get Spool but we need to let this play out. He's going somewhere; he's meeting someone. We want them all."

"No," I say. "What you're saying probably makes some sort of spy sense, but you don't have a sister. I'm sorry, Dale, but if you did, if you had a family, if someone you loved was in danger—we know Spool's a monster, we both know it—you wouldn't, you *couldn't* waste a second before you tried to save her."

There's an argument bubbling up inside him but he keeps his mouth closed and, for that, I like him more than ever.

"Floor it, car," he says.

The Smart Car weaves in and out of lanes until Spool's black Mercedes is in sight.

"Does he know we're creeping up on him?" I ask. "Does his car have the same spy doodads ours does?"

"That piece of junk?" sneers the car.

"He had to make a fast getaway," says Dale. "That's a standard unequipped vehicle. We have surprise on our side."

"Surprise!" I say, and open my door.

"What are you doing?" he yelps and grabs my arm. "Are you crazy?"

"You know the answer to that. Let me go."

"Bridget, you're not invincible. You're tough and you're fast but you've also been super lucky. So lucky that anyone who knows anything about luck would identify you as someone whose luck is about to run out."

"Dale, I want him to see my face. I want him to know that what he did to me, he's not doing to my sister."

"I'd let her go," says the car. "She crazy."

Dale sighs and opens the glove box. He hands me a tube of lip balm.

"Smoky pear," he says.

I kiss him. Real quick, on the lips. Maybe our teeth clash a little.

"For luck," I say.

"Ooooh," squeals the car.

"Get me close, close enough to smell what he had for breakfast," I snarl.

"Nice way to talk," says the car.

We pick up speed. The trunk of the Mercedes is in sight.

I shove the door of the Smart Car open. One glance back at Dale. "Take me out for doughnuts once this is over?"

He forces a smile.

"Take care of him, car."

"Take care of yourself," says the car.

I swing out of the driver's-side door and climb onto the roof of the car. I keep hold of the door and lever myself up. It takes me a second to get my balance. The wind is whipping in my face. I lurch from side to side. I hold my arms out to steady myself. The black Mercedes is maybe fifty yards ahead. I wait for the car to wipe twenty yards off that gap. Then I inch my way backward. There's barely room on the roof of this little car to give me much of a running start but my legs start pumping and my arms scythe through the air. I feel myself leave the roof.

My plan, if the mad scramble of thoughts whirring around my crazed panicky mind could be classified as a plan, was to land on the top of Spool's car, slide down onto the hood, and stare him full in the face, before . . . well, I hadn't worked out the next part, but I'm sure it would have been good. I did not, however, muster up enough power as I leaped from the Smart Car to land on Spool's roof. Instead, I free-fall toward the back of the car. I slam my palms down hard on the metal of the Mercedes trunk. It hurts and I feel my nails break as I try to cling on to the sides of the trunk and keep my balance. At the same time, I push my legs forward and kick both feet out in front of me as far and as hard as I can. The rear windshield shatters. The sudden wind blows fragments of glass back in my face. From inside the car, I hear Natalie scream.

"Natalie!" I try to yell back.

I manage to hook a leg inside the edge of the broken windshield, and that's the only thing keeping me from falling to the ground.

"Hi, Bridget," calls out Spool. He sounds unsurprised by my sudden appearance in the back window of his car.

"Bridget?" Natalie sounds stunned. "*My* Bridget?"

Aww.

"Hold on, Natalie, I'm coming," I shout. Although, having said that, I can't imagine at this point how I'm going to get into that car. My foot is barely hanging on to the inside of the window. I try to pull myself up. It's not happening. I'm not strong enough. The wind is blasting me full in the face and the car is moving too fast for me to get a strong enough grip. Dale was right. I should have waited. We could have surprised Spool. I pushed my luck and it ran out on me. One more try. I put everything I've got into pulling myself up. I feel the strain in my back. It hurts too much. I'm not going to make it. I'm going to slide off the trunk and be crushed under oncoming traffic. And then I see a hand.

It reaches out of the broken windshield.

"Bridget, get in," says Natalie. I drag myself up one more time, reach for her hand and, with an effort, she pulls me in. I tumble onto the backseat, breathless and dizzy. Natalie's eyes are wide and confused. "What are you doing at my audition?" she says.

Now I'm confused. "What are you talking about? Why would you get in a car with a complete stranger?"

"He's a well-known producer. He's had shows on Broadway. He knows talent when he sees it and that's what he sees in me. I'm getting ready for my song. What are you doing here?"

I've just kicked my way in through the back windshield of a Mercedes. The driver has fired a gun at me. My little sister is vexed by my presence, but not to the degree that it stops her from launching into her vocal warm-ups. I see Spool smirk in the rearview mirror.

"What did you do to her?" I shout.

"She's in a safe, happy place," he says. "She won't suffer any trauma and she gets to live out her dream. I could snap her out of it, though. If that's what you want. If you really believe she should know who you are."

"La la la la la la la," sings Natalie.

"Talented family," says Spool.

I want to shake Natalie, to make her see where she is and what's happening to us. But I don't want her to be scared.

"I can do it to your whole family," says Spool. "I can take you right out of the picture."

"Gosh, I'm nervous." Natalie laughs. "But it's the

good kind of nervous. I hope he likes me."

Spool has one hand on the wheel. He keeps glancing back at me, a half smile on his face. "Wouldn't it be better for your whole family if you were gone? Wouldn't it be better for you?"

I think of all the lies I've told since I became a spy, all the fights and arguments I've caused.

"You were almost invisible before, Bridget. Go all the way now. Do it for them. Look at her face."

I look. The nervous, excited smile is still in place. But I see tears glistening at the corners of her eyes. Part of her knows something isn't right here. Part of her is fighting. She was perfect and I've put her in this vulnerable situation. I made her a target. I hate Spool with every fiber of my being, but I can't say he doesn't have a point.

"Let me help," he says.

"Yeah, like I want you poking around in my family's heads," I say.

I put a hand over Natalie's mouth and nose, then I pull out my lip balm and aim it at Spool.

"See how you like being invisible."

I fire. The car doesn't fill with smoke. A laser beam shoots out and burns a hole straight through the windshield. I scream in fright. So does Natalie. So does Spool. So it's *one* twist for laser and *two* twists for smoke?

Spool pulls out a gun. I fire again, burning his hand, causing him to drop the gun. Which is good but also bad because now he's lost control of the car. The Mercedes skids wildly across lanes. Cars around us honk and tires screech as motorists swerve to avoid us. I tug a seat belt around Natalie.

"Sing, Nat!" I yell. Anything to keep her safely in her fantasy world while the real one is falling apart around us. She begins to warble. A few weeks ago, I would have been annoyed and intimidated that she's so good at everything she does. Now I'm enraged that she has a gift and a psychotic pink-faced monster exploited it to get me back in his clutches.

Sirens start to wail. Two police motorcycles are chasing after us.

Spool drags the Mercedes into the nearest lane, cutting right in front of a UPS van, missing it by inches.

I lean forward. "Spool, do you get what's happening here? You're kidnapping minors. You're being chased by police vehicles. There's going to be reporters and helicopters. You're going to be on TV. Your face is going to be out there. It's over for you."

"I keep forgetting you're just a child," he says.

"And you know how children love being talked down to," I retort.

"It's never over for people like me. You think there aren't agents all around the world who would willingly sell out their own countries—their own families—to align themselves with me? You think there aren't a hundred other Carter Strikes out there? There are, and they may not want to admit it, but they need people like me. Because people like your father? They're bullets. Deadly but useless. Me? I'm the gun."

Spool slams his foot down and tries to put as much distance as possible between the Mercedes and the cops. I'm thrown back in my seat. Natalie stops singing. "Was that okay?" she asks, her face hopeful. "I have other songs, if you'd like to . . ." She trails off, waiting for someone to respond.

I look at my sister. Then I look at Spool, knuckles white on the wheel, muttering to himself.

They're both trapped in fantasies. Spool thinks he's still the master manipulator, *still* two steps ahead of everyone else. He has plans unfolding in his head. New alliances to make, new enemies to crush, new agents to entrap. What a loser! He changes lanes again. This time, he smashes the headlight of a van he doesn't quite manage to avoid. That's when I know he's going to get us killed, and he doesn't care because he's deep inside his own world where he's still in charge.

"I wish I'd never met you, Bridget," he barks. "I wish I'd never found out you existed. You and your father have given me nothing but trouble."

"You, on the other hand, have been a complete joy, Spool," I reply. "Nothing but good times."

"But I'm not letting you go," he says. "We're going to start a new Section 23 from scratch, you and me."

"No, thanks. I saw what you did with the last one."

"You don't have a choice."

"I do," I say. "And I choose to let you continue your journey without me or my sister."

I point my lip balm straight up at the roof of the car. One click. The laser slices through.

"You might make it out," Spool says. "But her as well?"

"She's not going anywhere. Neither am I."

I start to circle my arm clockwise. The laser cuts through the rest of the roof, through the window, through the door, through the floor, separating me and Natalie from Spool.

He realizes what I'm doing. He lurches out of his seat and makes a grab at me. I kick up quickly and catch him under the chin. The force of my foot bangs Spool's head against the roof. He flops back down in his seat. I finish blasting the lip balm across the car. It takes a few more seconds than I thought. There's some ripping and tearing. Some buckling and bending of metal. And then . . .

. . . the front half of the car, Spool's half, wrenches itself away from the back half.

I see Spool stare at me in anger, disbelief, and what I like to think of as a little drop of admiration, as he tries to control the two-wheeled vehicle he's suddenly found himself driving.

The Mer—and it really is a Mer, me and Natalie are in the Cedes—pinballs across lanes, battering off oncoming vehicles. I'm so fixated on the fate of Spool's half car that I forget, briefly, that me and my sister, who is still marooned in an artificial alternate universe, are also in a two-wheeled vehicle, this one without any steering. We're basically stuck in a mobile gas tank that is careening wildly out of control.

"So should I go now?" says Natalie. "You've got my details?"

I undo her seat belt. This is going to be tricky. There's barely a roof to stand on and there are two of us. I really didn't think this through. I glance out the broken windshield. Gas is leaking from the tank. If we don't get out now, this thing is going up in a ball of fire. I grab Natalie's hand.

"I know you can hear me, Natalie. I know somewhere

in there, you know I'm with you. Follow me. Don't let go of my hand. Keep close to me. I'll keep you safe. Okay?"

"Okay," she says.

My plan is to leap onto the hood of the next vehicle that passes and pull Natalie along with me. Again, not fully thought through. Am I strong enough to keep hold of her? What if I underestimate the jump and bounce off the car? What if Natalie lets go?

"Stop wasting time and jump!" I hear my voice command.

Except it's not my voice. It's the Smart Car.

The little car has pulled up parallel to the Cedes. Dale hangs out the door, an arm open.

"You can do this," I tell Natalie.

I push her toward the open door. "Reach out, Nat!" I yell.

Whatever part of Natalie that isn't submerged reaches out an arm. Dale takes it and pulls her into the Smart Car.

I gasp in relief. Time to go. I look over at the car. There isn't room for three people in there. Guess I'm headed up to the roof. I get ready to jump but a hand grabs my wrist and pulls me back.

"I told you I wasn't letting you go," croaks Spool.

I yelp in shock and glance behind me. Well, I can't

talk about his pink face anymore. What's glaring at me is like a hunk of steak that's been barbecued a few minutes past charred. He's still alive, though. The tenacious little critter.

He tries to clamp his burned and blackened hands around my throat. I bring my knee up to my chest and push him back. He's strong, though, strong and determined. I don't know if I can keep him at bay. The longer Spool's hands grope at the air around my face, the more I smell burning flesh. I close my eyes so I don't have to see his horrific face. Just as he's about to overpower me, I feel a bump. The Smart Car bangs into the side of my half car. Dale is hanging out with his arm outstretched.

I hear him shouting, "Bridget, jump!"

I want to. I want to jump to Dale, to Natalie, even to the stupid car with my voice.

But the position I'm in makes it impossible to move. Spool just seems to get stronger. And I smell the fuel leaking out of the tank. I think maybe I got more than my fair share of luck and it finally ran out.

But at least I know who I am and I know what I can do. I know what matters to me. I know I'd do anything for my family. I know how to be a better friend. And I kissed somebody. And I met my real father. Something I didn't even know I wanted. That's pretty good.

I feel my strength ebbing away. I feel my knees giving way under the strain of keeping Spool away from me. I feel his blackened hands touch my throat. I hear Dale scream my name. I hear Natalie scream my name. Then I hear Carter Strike scream my name.

"Bridget!" he yells, his voice now louder than the others.

I open my eyes.

Strike is on a motorcycle reversing at high speed toward the half car. He jumps up on the seat of the cycle, spins around, leans forward, grabs me, and pulls me out of Spool's clutches. Then he spins back around, deposits me behind him, pulls my arms around his waist, and turns the motorcycle around.

"You've got amazing moves for a guy your size," I say once again, because it may be a little insensitive but it's true.

There's an enormous explosion behind us. The air turns hot. Fragments of jagged metal shower down.

I turn to look back.

"Don't," says Strike.

So I don't.

CHAPTER THIRTY-FOUR

We Are Family

"Mr. and Mrs. Wilder, my name is Carter Strike. I've been looking forward so much to meeting you. Obviously, I envisaged the circumstances being a little different."

Strike smiles at my freaked-out parents. He also smiles at the small platoon of police who'd been staking out our house since the mysterious phone call from an Inspector Carr, of whose existence the Sacramento Police Department have no record.

Strike gives me a reproachful look. The look we discussed when it was agreed he'd throw me under the bus.

"This one. This troublemaker. I thought she had your permission. I had no idea, I promise you, that she sought me out without discussing it with you first."

His sincerity, his awkwardness, his chubby frame and the ill-fitting suit barely containing it all contribute to making Mom and Dad a little less horrified by the stranger who showed up at their door with the daughter they only now realize has been missing most of the day.

"She's a smart one, our Bridget," continues Strike with a rueful headshake. "But thinking before she acts? Not one of her strongest attributes. Not yet, anyway."

"Not like Natalie here," breaks in Dale, who is standing next to and sort of propping up my dazed sister. "If it wasn't for her I'd probably still be in that rehearsal hall waiting for that so-called producer, if he even existed. But she was all, 'This is a scam. We're out of here.' You raised a sensible, responsible young lady here."

"Scam" is about all Natalie is able to say. Once the selective memory injection Strike gave her makes its presence felt, she'll be far more articulate and outraged about the fake producer who wasted her talent and her time.

"Okay," says the sergeant from the Sacramento Police Department. "You can confirm that these are your daughters?"

"Yes," Mom and Dad both say.

"And you know the men who brought them home?"

"No," Mom and Dad both say.

"Do you want to press charges?"

Mom and Dad look at each other.

"If I were in your situation, I'd have the exact same hesitation," says Strike. "You don't know me. You don't know the kind of man I am, what kind of secrets I may be harboring. All I can tell you is a few days ago, I was a reasonably successful rug importer . . ."

Strike passes Mom his phone. The screen has a picture of him standing proudly outside a rug warehouse.

". . . who lived an uncomplicated life. Then I got an email and a phone call from someone claiming to be my daughter. And suddenly my life got complicated."

Mom and Dad look at me, their eyes tearing up. "Why didn't you say something? Why didn't you come to us?" says Mom.

"We always said we'd help you find your real parents if that's what you wanted," says Dad.

The tears filling up my eyes aren't fake. I rehearsed this with Strike but I never knew how awful it was going to feel.

"I should have talked to you. I'm sorry," I mumble.

Dad gives the SPD sergeant a *We'll take it from here* nod. The cops shuffle back to their cars. Dad pulls me in for a hug. Mom grabs us both. She reaches out and pulls Natalie in, too.

"I know you girls are growing up. I know you need your own space. I get that you want to feel like you're independent," says Mom. "But when it's important, when it's something that really matters, don't ever feel that you can't come to us, that we won't make time."

"I won't," I say, wiping my eyes.

"Won't either," says Natalie.

We start to walk back to the house. Dad turns around.

"Mr. Strike. Would you like to come in?"

Strike looks taken aback and unsure how to proceed. I don't think he's faking it. We didn't plan a strategy beyond getting me home.

Mom walks back to him. "You're Bridget's family. You're going to be a part of our family, which, I know, is a scary prospect. Come in, Carter."

A very bashful-looking Strike allows my mom to walk him toward our house. I can hear her telling him about my flute. This is going to be nothing but embarrassing.

I glance at the driveway. Dale is walking away. Alone.

"I'll be right back," I tell Mom and Strike. "I just want to thank that kid for getting Nat home safe. That was super nice of him."

I run after Dale.

"Really?" I say. "Just like that? Without a word? Am I going to see you in school?"

He looks uncomfortable. "I'm an awesome hacker. Even if I'm not working for Strike, I'm getting offers."

"Remember that conversation we had about you walking away from the whole spying-slash-hacking thing?"

"I wish I could," he says.

"Then do it. There's a buzz about you in school. You're the guy who shoved Brendan Chew. You can build on that."

Dale smiles. "That may have been my finest hour."

I frown. "So that kiss wasn't in any way memorable?"

He glances back at my house. The front door is open. No parents or Strike in sight.

"Other than worrying that you might die in a ball of fire, it's been the only thing on my mind," he says.

And by the way he kisses me, I'm inclined to believe him.

Then I hear a distant "Oooooh!" that gets louder as the stupid Smart Car rolls into view.

Dale pulls away from me. He gets into the car.

For a second, we look at each other from behind the windshield. Then the image changes. He fades away and there's an anonymous guy behind the wheel.

I watch the car drive away and wonder if I'll ever see Dale Tookey again.

I start to walk back to the house when I hear a car come to a halt.

Dale.

He came back.

"Bridget Wilder?"

He didn't come back. It's the sergeant from the Sacramento Police Department.

"We have your brother, Ryan, in custody. He stole a Korean barbecue food truck."

CHAPTER THIRTY-FIVE

Visible

Last night ended with us going to get Ryan out of the holding cell. Again. But I don't care, because this morning I'm having a normal family breakfast with my normal family. With one difference. I'm part of it.

"Bridget, do you think Carter would like Lisa?" Lisa is Mom's always-single, no-luck-with-men friend.

"Don't answer that, Bridget," says Dad. "Carter still has a good opinion about us. We don't want that to change just yet."

"Do you think he'd want to come to Raging Waters with us?" Mom asks.

"Mom, he's a busy guy."

"But we can still go, right? It's not too soon since the last time?" says Dad.

Look, I know they're overcompensating because they think they might lose me. The truth is, they won't. Ever. But I also know this be-nice-to-Bridget campaign isn't going to last forever, so I'm going to get what I can out of it.

"Hmmm," I say. "Let me check my schedule. Perhaps I can fit in another trip to this Raging Waters of which you speak."

"Raging Waters," squeals Natalie. "Are we going back? I can't wait. Isn't that the best news ever, Bridget?"

She rushes up and hugs me. I tense for the inevitable Whisper of Doom. It does not come. Instead, she pulls away and gives me a big, beaming smile, her eyes shining.

"Can we walk to school together? We never do that."

"Let her check her schedule," says Dad, cracking himself up.

I'm being made fun of in a nice way. I said something and it was remembered enough to become a joke. Maybe this whole be-nice-to-Bridget thing will last. Maybe I'm making it easier to be nice to me.

"So," says Natalie as we stroll to school. "That guy . . ."
Uh-oh.

"The one who waited with me at the fake audition. He goes to Reindeer Crescent, right?"

Again, uh-oh.

"I can't remember his name. Which is weird because we spent all that time together."

"Well, what did you talk about? Did he tell you anything about himself?"

Natalie looks confused. I know why and it kills me. But I've got to move her away from this subject. "I can't remember. It's making me mental. I remember everything, but this guy . . . it's like there's nothing."

She taps a finger off her forehead for emphasis.

"So what does that tell you?" I say carefully. "He made no impression. He had a chance to dazzle the soon-to-be-famous Natalie Wilder and he blew it."

Natalie giggles.

"Listen, Nat, you're going to meet a lot of boys. The ones that matter, you remember *everything* about them. What they say, what they do, what they wear, how they kiss . . ."

"Bridget, oh my God, you said kiss!" screeches Natalie. "Are you speaking from *kiss*perience? Do you have *kiss*tory?"

I go red and stammer, "I . . . I . . . I . . ." I'm half playing up my discomfort to get her mind off the subject of the boy she thinks she met at the fake audition and I'm half acutely embarrassed because I totally lost myself thinking about Dale, who is, of course, the boy she thinks she met at the fake audition.

"Today on the Conquest Report. The Wilder sisters seen plotting and conspiring. Watch your backs, Reindeer Crescent."

Joanna walks along with us. "Ladies," she says, and gives me a knowing look.

I don't know what to think about her knowing look. The bruise on her forehead where Xan whacked her is fading, but it must be a constant reminder to Joanna. Strike told me she was gone once he made it out of the grille so presumably her memory is intact. But what she knows and what she's storing up to use against me is a big scary question mark. Maybe we share a secret and it's finally given us a reason to continue our friendship.

"What's the latest juice on the little sister network, young Wilder?" Joanna asks Natalie. "I'll keep your name out of it."

Natalie looks back over her shoulder, then leans in close to Joanna. "Well," she breathes.

I don't even listen. I'm walking to school with my

friend and my sister. It's never happened before, but I hope it happens again.

A white SUV comes to a stop at the light up ahead. As we draw close, Mrs. Breakbush gives me a faint smile. I glance at the backseat. Casey, Kelly, and Nola are all staring at their phones, ignoring one another.

"Keep running," I mouth at Mrs. Breakbush. "You look good."

She seems surprised but smiles back and mouths, "Thank you."

"The light's not getting any greener, *Mom*," says Casey. I give Mrs. Breakbush a sympathetic wave as she drives away.

"Midget Wilder goes to the doctor," says Brendan Chew as I walk into A117. "Says, Doctor, I've got a problem. He says, I can't see you right now." Chew glances at his disinterested audience. "'Cause she's so small," he explains.

I stroll up to Chew and pull back my arm. He flinches. I run a hand through my hair. Ha!

"Nice flinch," I say. "This midget just made you pee your big-boy pants."

"The midget made him pee his big-boy pants!" echoes around A117. Fingers tap furiously on phones.

Chew shrivels in his seat. It wasn't even that funny but the timing was everything.

C, K & N walk into A117 looking at their phones. They glance up, take the temperature of the room. Chew's cold. I'm hot.

"Hi, Bridget," they chorus.

I nod back. Just enough to acknowledge their presence. Not enough to show I care. I bet I get an invitation to eat lunch with them today. But I'm not going unless Joanna comes, too. And they're serving corn on the cob.

Today is just one day. I'm not going to be as cool, confident, and in control every day. But I'm not going back to what I was, either. I've seen too much. I've done too much. I know too much. I'm somebody now. Somebody special.

Acknowledgments

I would like to thank my agent, Tina Wexler; my editor, Maria Barbo; and also Lori Majewski, James Greer, Tad Floridis, Jordanna Fraiberg, and everyone at Katherine Tegen Books.

Bridget Wilder will return in

Bridget Wilder
Spy to the Rescue

"I am not a spy," I say with what I hope is the right mixture of innocence, irritation, and confusion.

The six cheerleaders who kidnapped me regard me with cold, hostile, disbelieving eyes.

If I was any sort of spy, I would not have been so easily bamboozled by the tall, willowy blond girl who sidled up to me as I was heading home from Reindeer Crescent Middle School and held a tiny, big-eyed kitten out to me.

"Isn't he beautiful?" the willowy blonde said in a baby voice. "Isn't he the most adorable ball of fluff you've ever seen?"

As if on cue, the little gray kitten reached out a paw to me.

"He *loves* you," the blond girl almost sang. "He wants to go home with you. Here. Nuzzle him."

My gurgly-voiced new friend thrust the kitten into my hands. Feeling him squirm and adjust himself in my grip made me melt a little inside.

"Take him home," urged the blonde. "Be good to him. Give him the love he needs. He'll give it back to you a hundred times over."

There were a million reasons to say no. My mom hates cats. My dad is allergic. My brother can't be trusted not to sit on them. It would immediately fall in love with my little sister and ignore me. I'd have to feed him and clean up after him but . . . those big eyes . . . the way he smooshes up against me. The thought hit me: *Am I a cat person? I think I am!*

I nodded at the blonde. She let out a sigh of contentment, hooked her arm through mine, and guided me toward a school bus parked a few yards away from the others.

"Jump in here and I'll give you his collar and his toys, and then this wonderful kitten will be all yours."

"In there?" I should have said. "Why is a cat's collar and toys in a school bus?" I should have said. "By the way, who are you, tall, willowy, blond girl?" I should have said. But I was fully focused on the little gentleman squirming in my arms as I climbed the steps into the bus.

The second I was inside, my spy senses clicked into gear. This bus was no refuge for abandoned cats. It was filled with cheerleaders. There were six of them, including the willowy blonde who had lured me onto the bus, all dressed in little pleated skirts and tight blue crop tops bearing the Bronze Canyon Valkyries logo, all displaying enviable abs, all looking like they wanted to rip my head off.

The bus door closed behind me.

"Hit it!" snarled the blonde.

The occupant of the driver's seat, a horse-faced woman somewhere in her late twenties, pulled the bus away from the school.

"Give me that," said the blonde as she yanked the kitten from my hands.

I sized up the situation. The no-longer-baby-voiced blonde stroked the mewling kitten and barred the door. The other five cheerleaders stood in what I would later discover to be bowling-pin formation in the aisle, making escape impossible.

"Where are we going?"

"Santa Clarita," growled the driver. "To Bronze Canyon Academy. The school you tried to blackmail."

"I what?" I said, nonplussed.

The girl at the tip of the bowling pin, the one with blinding white teeth and hair tied up in a huge polka-dotted bow, thrust her phone in my face. I saw cheerleaders flipping and tumbling. To be more specific, I saw Reindeer Crescent's own Cheerminator squad filmed, in somewhat shaky fashion, mid-practice.

I darted a glance out the window nearest me. The bus was traveling in the opposite direction of my route home.

A finger snapped in my face. "Hey!" barked Big Bow. "Eyes on the screen." I felt a thin wire of anger begin to pulse in me. I looked back at the phone which now displayed an email. I had to lean in so close to read it my glasses almost touched the screen. But I managed to make out the text: *Pay me $1200 & you'll get the rest of the choreography b4 the Cheerminators premiere it at Classic Cheer.*

The bus juddered around a corner. I stumbled forward, almost falling into Big Bow. She took a step back. The two rows of Valkyries behind her stepped back at the same time. I grabbed onto a seat to get my balance.

"Ladies," I said, trying to remain calm. "I think there's been a mistake. I think what's going on here is Cheer Business, and, even if being an awesome judge of character isn't a required Valkyrie skill, if you spend a quarter of a second looking at me, it ought to be blindingly clear I don't care about Cheer Business."

"Your name does," said one of the Mid-Pin girls.

Once again, I was forced to squint at the screen. The email was sent by someone known as *Bird Tweet Girl*.

"Don't cheereotype us," said Big Bow. "Being an awesome judge of character is a required Valkyrie skill. In fact, we look for a whole range of talents. One of which is the ability to rearrange letters to form other words."

"Anagrams," I said.

"Cheerleaders love anagrams," she declared. "For instance, if you rearrange the letters of Bird Tweet Girl, you get . . ."

"Bridget Wilder." I nodded. "You also get Driblet Red Wig, Bed Dig Twirler, Bridled Wet Rig, and Brr Weed Dig Lit." I used to be very into making anagrams of my name before I was cool like I am now. (My record was two hundred. I know there's a *lot* more.)

"But mainly you get Bridget Wilder," scowled Big Bow. She folded her arms in triumph. Behind her, the two rows of Valkyries folded their arms in unison.

"You think *I* sent you an email demanding money for footage of the new Cheerminator choreography?"

The Valkyries nodded in unison.

"Motive!" shouted the willowy blonde. "Your sister's

a new Cheerminator."

This was true. My younger sister Natalie had, on a whim, tried out for the Cheerminators a month earlier, and like the effortless overachiever and automatic center of attention she is, instantly became the high-flying jewel in its crown.

"You conspired with her to cut out the competition," accused Big Bow.

"You're a spy for the Cheerminators," said the driver. "You're trying to get us to buy the footage and then you'll report us to the Cheer Classic competition committee and get us disqualified for contravening the rules."

"I am not a spy," I say. Which is where we came in.

"Only someone who is a spy would say something like that," yells the willowy blonde. She takes the kitten's paw and claws the air with it. "This cat hates you."

"I'm being set up," I tell the Valkyries. "I didn't send the email. I didn't film the practice. I don't want your money."

"What do you think, Coach?" Big Bow calls over to the driver. "She made a pretty convincing case. Should we turn around and take her back to her school?"

The driver taps her fingers off her chin. "Mmmmm . . . ," she ponders. "No."

Big Bow puts a hand on my shoulder and goes

to shove me down in the nearest seat. "Relax, Bridget Wilder. You're going to be here for a while. We're taking you back to our school. You're going to confess in front of the entire faculty and student body so that they know our cheer-tegrity is intact!"

"Shouldn't that be cheer-tact?" I ask. Big Bow acts like she didn't hear me.

I make a quick scan of the bus. Blonde and kitty still block the front door. Bowling-pin formation stands between me and the rear exit. That leaves windows to my right and left. Am I fast and limber enough to jump toward them, open the locks, and slide out?

You never know if you don't try.